JESSICA MOORE

Pirates, Wenches & Murder

A Susie Carter Mystery

Jessica Moore

Published by Next Page Press.

First published in April 2018 by Next Page Press.

DEDICATION

Dedicated to Mum & Sue.
Thanks for your ongoing support.

FREE MYSTERY BOOKS

Love a good Murder Mystery?

If so join our newsletter list and receive free murder mystery books and updates from Next Page Press including new release news.

www.NextPagePress.com

1

TENSION FILLED THE AIR AS HE DREW THE GUN from its leather holster. This wasn't just an ordinary gun either. This was an old-fashioned flintlock gun you might see in an old pirates movie from the 1950's. The type you had to stuff the gun powder into with a rod.

He waved the gun menacingly toward his intended victim.

Susie gasped and held her breath.

'Give me one reason why I shouldn't do it then?' he screamed. Every word laced with anger.

James Foley was on his knees and had a look of terror in his eyes. This wasn't the way he had expected his life would end. But now he was out of luck.

He had no bargaining chips left.

He was out of luck and he knew it.

So he resigned himself to the inevitable.

'Good sir I beg of you, if you are to shoot me dead then at least let the women go.'

The intruder looked around at the two terrified women standing behind Foley. He had no mind to be letting them go. In fact, he had other plans for them he thought causing a wicked smile to flood his face.

Susie gasped again. She read his mind and became horrified at the thought.

'And why should I let them go?'

He was toying with them all now. The rum he had been drinking all day was causing him to be a little unsteady on his feet. The gun waving from side to side. Still, he was dangerous and unpredictable.

'They mean nothing to you.' James pleaded for their lives.

'Aye, but they are a fine pair. I could put them into service.'

'Good sir I assure you they are not good workers. The fat one is lazy, and the other is too old to be of any use to you. Please let them be.'

'Silence!'

Beads of sweat filled James's forehead. It trickled off and ran down the side of his face.

The intruder cocked the gun and steadied himself as he aimed the gun at his temple. He was sick of this grovelling fool and his two wenches. It was time to do what he had come for. It was time to do what he had come for. To take what was his.

'Tell me where the gold is before I blow you into an early grave?'

'But sir, I don't have the gold you speak of.'

'Don't fool with me. I know you took it. I be seeing you around the ports snooping around the Fortune Hunter.'

The Fortune Hunter had been at dock for the last week. Back from a six month stint in the Caribbean it brought back gold, coffee and cocoa supplies from the islands. It was rumored that the captain kept a stash of gold hidden in the hull. What wasn't known is the curse of death placed over the one who might dare to touch it.

James Foley was now learning just how real the curse was proving to be.

'True, I was down by the ports. But only to offer a warm bed for the night to a weary sailor.'

'And where be these weary sailors then?'

'None came, sir.'

'Enough of this nonsense.' He screamed in a rage. 'If you won't show me the gold, then I will kill you all.'

Susie screamed in terror.

The fat one pulled open a draw where she hid an old tobacco tin. She pulled the lid off to reveal four pounds in change. Her life savings.

She held it out to the intruder. 'Here. Take it.'

He took a step forward and reached out with his left hand.

His right hand fell by his side. The gun dangling down.

James knew it was now or never. This was his opportunity.

A moment of hesitation and then he leapt to his feet straight into the intruder pushing him back against the wall. A struggle followed as each man attempted to get the upper hand.

BANG!

The flintlock fired.

A smell of gunpowder filled the air.

James Foley took two steps backwards. His hands clasped to his gut.

He swung around to one side to face the women with a sorry look in his eyes. The pain overwhelming him he dropped to one knee, then collapsed in a heap on the floor. His body twitched and rolled in agony for a moment. Then nothing. Motionless.

The ladies eyes filled with tears at losing him.

'And Cut!' yelled the director.

A round of applause broke out across the theatre.

'Marvelous people. Just marvelous.' Irvine Maxwell cried out, clapping his hands in an overtly gay fashion. 'Everything has come together so wonderfully. I think we are ready for opening night.'

Further applause filled the room as the cast and crew wrapped up their final dress rehearsal. Opening night for the Castaways musical was now just days away. Everything seemed in order.

Irvine Maxwell had done a marvellous job in getting everyone on track for opening night. With only a months rehearsal the play had come together he thought to himself. It helped to have an ex-Hollywood star as his leading man.

Maxwell was a small time director who spent the last couple of decades directing B grade theatre in London's West end.

Celebrated for his work with The Other Cats he had a long and distinguished career. Five years ago he retired to a little cottage overlooking the sea in Marazion. He still loved the theatre though and relished the opportunity to direct Castaways each year as part of the Pirates & Wenches Convention.

'Okay everyone. Remember we have our cast and crew dinner tonight at six.' Maxwell reminded them. The traditional dinner before opening night was his least favourite part of the theatre, but it helped to create a certain comradery amongst the team.

With that he headed out the back to the green room where he poured himself a gin and tonic. He slumped into the old leather couch with glass in hand and wondered if this would be his last time directing the theatre.

A door slammed to the side of the green room. Maxwell knew what the trouble was. Same as always. Karl Lightfoot, who played the part of the intruding pirate, was bellowing about the part of the intruding pirate, was bellowing about the overacting of James Foley the leading man.

Maxwell just laughed to himself and finished his drink crunching on the ice at the end. In all his years in the theatre the one constant was drama between the actors. It went with the territory and Castaways had proved no different.

Karl and James had been at each other since the first day of rehearsal and it was likely to carry on long after the final curtain call.

Maxwell finished his drink and headed back to his cottage to freshen up.

2

The Smugglers Inn was the venue for the cast and crew dinner. Patty Malone had owned the pub for many years. Part of a family tradition. The pub had a long history as one of the first buildings in Polmerton.

It was a classic Cornish style building extended throughout the years.

In days gone by the Smugglers Inn was the centre of town activities. Local fishermen would board in the rooms out the back of the pub, and would frequent the bar looking for hot food and a pint of ale.

And more than the odd pirate ship or two had docked in port. When that occurred pirates took over the Smugglers Inn. The locals would make themselves scarce until they departed for richer pickings.

As the centre of town activities for many years the Smugglers Inn was extended, over one hundred and fifty years ago, to include a small theatre room out the back. It was complete with a stage, a green room for the cast, and seating for a hundred people if you packed them in tight.

Smugglers Inn was the venue for the annual Pirates & Wenches Convention play. This year the chosen play was the musical 'Castaways' which promised a swashbuckling good time for all.

As the host and publican Patty Malone had agreed to playing the part of Wench One in the play. And a fine wench she made too. In her early forties with the spirit of Ireland running through her veins she threw herself into the role with gusto.

She was a buxom woman with a jolly laugh. Her smile could light up a room and frequently she had the locals in fits of laughter as she made a wisecrack or two.

The opportunity to be in Castaways brought a little excitement to her life. And brought in some extra patronage to the pub she called home which was always welcome.

And she loved to be playing alongside her wench counterpart, and a relative newcomer to Polmerton, Lady Susie Carter. Patty decided Susie was a good sport for saying yes to the part and they had a jolly good time during the rehearsals.

Lady Susie Carter was talked into playing the part of Wench Two. She accepted after encouragement from her assistant Meg Lane, and business partner Hunter McGill.

Once she had the part, though she threw herself into it. No point doing things by half she told Megs.

Being such a good sport had endeared herself to the locals of Polmerton which was a good thing given the recent fiasco at Ash Castle. The Pirates & Wenches Convention had come at the right time. It had given everyone something else to focus on besides the murder of Mayor Abigail McGill at the opening night of the Cornish Cooking School.

Susie & Meg took great comfort in having something else to focus on. So they threw themselves into the organising of the convention and the play.

Megs had agreed to play the role of the young bride of the local police officer in the play. It was fitting given her crush on Constable Daniels. The role itself was a small one yet vital to the plot.

Susie and Megs arrived at the Smugglers Inn at ten minutes before six. The sign on the door informing them that this was the venue for the 'Castaways Cast & Crew Dinner.'

They opened the heavy old wooden door that creaked on its hinges. Stepping down through the entry they were greeted by a round of cheers. It was customary for those already arrived to greet each new arrival at the dinner with a hearty cheer.

Susie glanced around and by her reckoning at least half of the those to attend had already arrived and were sampling some of the finest Ale in Cornwall already.

Patty came across and gave both Susie and Megs a welcoming hug.

'I see you are still in your wenches outfit then?' joked Susie.

'Oh aye, I make a fine wench I do.' Patty roared with laughter.

'And a jolly good publican.' Susie added. And she was right. If anyone was more suited to the life of a publican in a small Cornish fishing village Susie was yet to meet them.

'Now would you like a glass of celebratory champagne?' Patty asked them. She was handing them each a glass before they had time to consider a response.

'Cheers!' they all said in unison.

Irvine Maxwell appeared through the door that lead back to the small theatre. He was dressed flamboyantly, with a purple silk shirt decorated with florals. His tight hugging white pants clung to his lean physic for dear life and flowed down to his alligator skin boots.

He spotted Susie and Megs and headed over to them sashaying through the crowd.

'Susie darling.' He said planting a kiss on her cheek. 'And the lovely Megs.'

'Wonderful to see you again Irvine.' Susie replied.

She had enjoyed working with Irvine Maxwell. To her, and no doubt the rest of the crew, his experience had shone through. In effect he had taken a bunch of everyday people who had never acted before and pulled off the miraculous. In less than four weeks the play had come together, and they were ready for opening night.

Patty handed a glass of champagne to Irvine.

'Heres to you Mr Irvine Maxwell for a job well done.'

A round of cheers filled the bar.

'Oh all the hard work is done, and now we can let the fun begin.' He shouted.

Another round of cheers as the drinks flowed.

A clap of thunder outside shook the Smugglers Inn as the rain came down. A typical spring day Patty informed them as they made small talk.

The old wooden door burst open catching everyone's attention in the bar. It had the desired effect as James Foley made his entrance. He presented himself at the door with all the glamour of a Hollywood star.

In his mind he still was.

The fact he hadn't been in anything of significance since he was eleven never held him back from feeling like a star. He was a classic case of the child star who's career never continued once the cute child looks disappeared.

Once a star always a star he told anyone who would listen.

And as the leading man in Castaways he made sure everyone knew who the star of the production was.

'My good people of Polmerton.' He bellowed in dramatic fashion. He had their attention, and he would not waste it.

'I have arrived so you may admire and adore me.'

There was a half hearted round of cheers in response as everyone got back to their conversations.

Behind the bar Mandy rolled her eyes. She couldn't stand James Foley. Last year at this same event she had given him a piece of her mind. Yet it didn't register with him. His out-of-control ego prevented him from hearing any feedback that wasn't laced in adoration. Even from his estranged daughter.

She had hated him from a young age. He knew it but didn't care.

A little miffed that his grand entrance didn't receive the height of adoration he had expected, James decided he needed a drink or two to get him in the mood to associate with these common folks. It was one of the many demands placed upon a star such as himself he would often tell himself.

Taking a champagne from a passing waitresses tray James made his way to where Irvine, Susie & Meg were standing.

'The party can start now I have arrived.' He stated. His voice rich and resonate bounced around the old bar drowning out most of the chatter nearby.

'Welcome James.' Susie said.

'James darling.' Irvine said with a fake joy. They air kissed and hugged. The two of them had a love hate relationship which Irvine described as they loved to hate each other.

Karl Lightfoot had been at one end of the bar knocking back the ales. With a good many under his belt he decided now would be a good time to say his heartfelt thanks to Irvine for everything, and to address one or two issues with the cast.

Standing up from the bar stool Karl's head span a little more than he expected. How many ales had he had he wondered? He remembered being the first to arrive, and he had been knocking them back for a good hour. Still, it couldn't have been more than a couple he decided as he made his way through the crowd.

As Karl approached Irvine and James he started to clap and shouting bravo much to the surprise of everyone. James, thinking it could only be for him, took a bow. Karl stopped clapping and glared at James but he didn't notice.

'Three cheers for our heroic director.' Karl declared raising his glass.

And three cheers they gave him.

'Oh stop please,' Irvine blushed, 'Don't stop!'.

'Seriously though, Irvine you have done it again.' Karl said. 'You've pulled a bunch of non-actors into shape in a short time frame.'

'Well there is one real actor.' James piped in.

'I don't see any.' Karl spat back full of spite.

'Now boys lets all play nice for tonight.' Irvine stood between them. The one thing he prayed for was to get through the night without everyone turning against each other. The world of theatre and actors was always a volatile one. Full of larger-than-life personalities who had an equal dash of insecurities made for many a fiery encounter.

Patty Malone stood upon a crate in front of the bar. She decided now was the perfect time. She tapped a silver knife against her champagne glass to get everyone's attention. The conversations wound to a halt as everyone fixed their focus on Patty.

'Good people of Polmerton and beyond,' she started. 'A hearty welcome to the Smugglers Inn for the cast and crew diner.'

A joyous round of cheer went up amongst the bar.

'Diner is now served in the dining room so if you could all make your way inside we can get started.'

With that they all went back to their conversations. Patty, Mandy and Meg worked their way around the bar ushering everyone to move into the dining room and take their seats.

The main dining table seated twenty. Each place had a name card showing where to sit. Meg was to the left of Susie. The place on the right reserved for Hunter McGill.

'Where is Mr McGill then?' Meg asked Susie.

'I have no idea,' Susie replied. 'He should be here by now.'

His bakery, The Famous Polmerton Bakery, was across the road. He lived in the cottage out the back with the gorgeous courtyard and old English rose garden that Susie loved so much. So he didn't have far to come to make it to the diner.

Susie became increasingly worried the more she wondered where he was.

'He's probably delayed locking up the shop and all.' Meg suggested. 'Quite right dear.'

Once everyone found their allocated spots Patty stood up and chinked her glass once again.

'Ladies and gents, pirates and wenches, tonight we have a special treat I know you are all going to die for,' She joked.

Hearty laughter filled the dining room.

With that the doors burst open and into the room bounded a red haired portly pirate carrying trays of his soon to be famous Cornish pasties that the old folks called 'Turps, Tarts and Tince.'

He let out an 'Arrgghhh me maties' as he plonked the tray on the table. A patch over one eye and a stuffed parrot on his left shoulder completed the look of Red Beard The Pirate.

Following him in dressed in a wenches outfit was Aimee his shop assistant. She also carried in trays of the finest Cornish food known to man. Aimee placed the tray on the side table.

Always one for fun Hunter raced across to Aimee, embraced her and tilted her over sideways and planted a rum laden kiss on her check. She let out a shriek in keeping with her character.

Huge cheers and a round of applause erupted at both the show and the smell of the food.

Mandy who was still working in the main bar ensured that a steady flow of Ale for the pirates, and champagne for the wenches, continued to flow. And flow it did.

3

Opening night arrived sooner than Susie had expected. Her nerves had been mounting throughout the day. Now as she stood backstage waiting for the curtains to open, she found herself to be in a state.

She could hear the crowd building as the folks from the village of Polmerton filed in and took their seats. There was a buzz in the air. Everyone had been talking about the new resident at Ash Castle. They had all heard about the murder of the mayor, and everyone was talking about Lady Carter taking part in the Castaways play.

Susie peered out from the curtain and took in the scene.

Meg sat in the second row and gave her a cheerful wave. Her small part was not until the second act so she planned to watch the rest from the crowd. She waved back and smiled.

'Five minutes people,' she heard Irvine Maxwell cry out.

Susie decide she needed a glass of water and made her way to find one. She passed Janet Brown, a delightful lady, she thought to herself as she did. She was carrying a rather larger roll of material. Susie wondered if she would whip up a new dress backstage. She was carrying it with both hands as she came towards her.

'Hi Janet,' Susie said as she drifted by.

Janet returned her greeting. Susie was impressed by Janet who had put together all the costumes for the production. She was a dressmaker by trade yet volunteered her service for the Castaways play each year. Now as the opening grew closer Janet was down on hands and knees mending the hem of a dress.

Susie poured herself a water and drank a full glass.

'Feeling thirsty there Lady Carter?' James Foley asked her.

'Just a tad. Nerves I think,' she replied.

'Oh I never have nerves. No I was born for this. This is my moment,' he responded as if addressing a crowd. He wished her luck and wondered off to take his position on stage.

'Two minutes people,' Maxwell cried out, 'everyone take your positions.'

There was a flurry of activity as actors took their place on stage for the opening musical number. Susie had to admit to Meg during the week she enjoyed the group songs in the play. The dancing was a little too much, but she thought she was getting the hang of it.

The lights dimmed, and a hush came over the crowd. There was not an empty seat in the small theatre and people stood lining the back walls as the curtains drew back.

With a brief musical interlude the cast of 'Castaways' burst into song for the opening number 'Once a Jolly Pirate.' The enthusiastic crowd joined in from the opening line and sung at the top of their voices. Susie hadn't expected the whole crowd to get involved by singing along and she relaxed immediately.

Meg was beaming a wide grin at her as the opening song came to a close.

For the next fifty minutes the audience was in raptures as Castaways made them laugh, sing and cry. Finally, the climactic closing scene.

James Foley had stated at the cast and crew dinner he felt he was born for this moment, the final scene in Castaways, where he takes a bullet from a wayward pirate to save the two wenches.

Right on cue Foley lept to his feet and tackled the intruding pirate. There was a brief struggle and the old gun fired.

BANG!

The sound rang out over the heads of the gathered crowd and reverberated off the walls. Blood sprayed across the stage and covered three people in the front row.

Foley reeled in pain on the ground.

'You've done it now Lightfoot,' he groaned in agony.

The curtains closed, and the crowd went wild with appreciation. They all jumped to their feet and clapped and cheered.

On stage, now mostly in the dark, Foley cried out for help but wasn't heard over the enthusiastic crowd.

'Oh that was so realistic that gun shot.' A voice in the crowd said to her neighbor.

The cast gathered in a line and held hands waiting for the curtain to open back up so they could take a bow. There was nothing like a standing ovation Maxwell was fond of saying. Now lining up on stage Susie knew what he meant. It was quite exhilarating.

The curtains opened back up and the crew took a bow.

Foley remained curled up in a ball on the stage behind the line up. Blood had pooled around him and his face had gone white. He cried out again for help but he was drowned out by the raucous applause.

Irvine Maxwell was called up to the stage. He took his place in the center of the line up and took a solo bow first, then joined hands with the crew and they took a group bow. He hushed the crowd down.

'And ladies and gentleman, what about a round of applause for our leading man, James Foley?,'

The crowd clapped and cheered again. Susie noted a slight drop in the enthusiasm level as she looked around for him. It was only then she realised he was still laying curled up in a ball.

'You can get up now James,' Maxwell called out to the now motionless Foley.

'Stop overacting!' demanded Karl Lightfoot.

Still Foley didn't move. Life draining out of his body.

Patty Malone was first to react followed by Susie. She rushed over to the body of Foley and rolled him onto his back. Susie screamed but covered it with her hand.

'He's dead,' Lightfoot called out.

Someone in the crowd screamed and sent chills down the spine of most of the audience.

Maxwell motioned for the curtains to be closed at once. The lights came back on revealing the look of horror on the faces of the crowd.

'He's been murdered!' an audience member shrieked.

More screams could be heard as the crowd scrambled for the door.

Maxwell checked for a pulse but there was none. James Foley, childhood Hollywood star, was dead. Shot dead in front of a live audience in the final scene of Castaways.

4

Susie stood back in disbelief. She clutched her hands to her chest at the horror.

'No!' Janet Brown screamed when she realised Foley was dead. She pushed past those gathered around on stage and threw herself to the ground in despair. With her arms wrapped around Foley's motionless body she declared her love for him for all to hear.

Paddy Malone gasped with shock when it dawned on her what had just happened. Her first thought was how this was going to effect her business. Her second thought was to get the Inspector.

'Daddy!' a cry could be heard from someone running to the stage.

Susie turned in time to see Mandy Reed run up the stairs to the side of the stage. She crossed to the middle of the stage and also threw herself at the body.

'Right oh, now then!' Inspector Reynolds called out. He asked everyone to take a step back from the crime scene. Mandy and Janet were still both cradled over the body weeping.

'Constable, get these two back from the crime scene,' the Inspector instructed young Constable Daniels. The constable had been enjoying a night out with his sweetheart Meg. They had been seated in the audience in the second row to watch the show.

The constable dutifully extracted each of the weeping ladies off the body and asked them to stand well back. Patty comforted Mandy giving her a shoulder to cry on. Janet Brown went and sat on a stool to the side of the stage.

'Okay now, everybody stand well clear of the crime scene while we conduct a proper investigation now,' the Inspector called out. He instructed the constable to get a detailed witness statement from each of the witnesses.

Karl Lightfoot was in shock. He was still standing in the same position on stage as he had when he pulled the trigger. The pistol in his hand was still smoking and warm. As it dawned on him the magnitude of what had happened, he started to panic.

He waved the gun in the direction of the body and the officers and declared he didn't do it, and that it wasn't him.

'Right, start with him then!' the Inspector commanded the young constable.

Constable Daniels did as he was instructed. He walked over to Lightfoot and took the gun from him. He placed it carefully on a table at the back of the stage. His handy black note book and pen were at the ready as he began to question the dazed Lightfoot.

The constable asked Lightfoot for his account of events.

Susie listened in with great interest.

Lightfoot explained that he did what he had done in the ten rehearsals leading up to this moment. He acted out the scene as the intruding pirate, and then as the script called for, he pulled the trigger of the old pistol.

It was meant to have blanks in the gun like in rehearsals he explained. He tried to offer an explanation as to how the blanks could have been substituted for real bullets but he had none.

Susie watched his facial expressions change as he had the realisation that he was the one who pulled the trigger. Everyone saw it. It was a live audience of a hundred or more people.

'I didn't shoot anyone!' he cried out. 'Someone must have switched the bullets!'

Lightfoot looked around the stage for some support. Someone to agree with him. But none came.

'We all saw what happened!' Cecil Miller replied. Miller walked off the stage and into the actors green room at the back where Irvine Maxwell could be heard weeping uncontrollably.

'Mr Lightfoot, try to calm down, and just walk us through how you recall the events,' Susie suggested helping the young constable out.

'Right, yes!'

Lightfoot explained how the night unfolded. He said he arrived early to begin his pre-play warm up routine. Foley was already there and the two of them exchanged a few heated words. It was obvious to all they didn't like each other he said. The constable took detailed notes.

As the crowd built all the crew were nervous, he went on.

Midway through the play he noticed his hem line had come apart, so he called to Janet Brown to mend it at the side of the stage. Good job she did, he continued, finishing just as his final scene was about to commence.

Lightfoot told them how he loved to make the entrance as the intruding pirate as he got to burst through the door into the Inn with the old pistol leading the charge. Seconds before his cue he looked around for the pistol but couldn't find it.

He was in a panic. It was his moment about to be ruined by the lack of a prop.

Then as if by magic someone placed the pistol into his hand as he burst onto the stage.

'Who was it?' Susie asked.

'Who was what?'

'That placed the pistol into your hand?'

'I have no idea. What does it matter anyway? I pulled the trigger. I'm the one who killed him!'

Those gathered on the stage gasped at the confession.

Lightfoot broke down sobbing and was led to a chair to take a seat.

Susie followed Constable Daniels around as he took statements from everyone on stage. One by one they all pretty much told the same story from their various positions on stage. They all recalled the moment that Lightfoot pulled the trigger. Everyone thought Foley was overacting when he failed to stand and join his cast in taking a bow.

A forensics team had arrived and where in discussions with Inspector Reynolds. They had been examining the body in search of clues. Susie joined them and listened in as they discussed the fact that there was nothing out of the ordinary apart from the gun shot.

Numerous photos were taken of the body. The pistol was placed into a large plastic bag to be reviewed back at forensics lab.

Everyone watched as the body was lifted and placed into a body bag. The sound of the zipper doing up made it all too real for them.

Irvine Maxwell re-appeared on the stage. It seemed obvious to Susie that he had been drinking heavily backstage and weeping at the same time. He looked a wreck, and he was highly emotional.

'You killed my star!' he screamed at Lightfoot and lunged at him.

He managed to get his hands to his throat as the forward momentum knocked Lightfoot off the stool and they both tumbled to the ground. Cecil tried in vain to break them up as they wrestled on the ground.

'That's enough!' Inspector Reynolds cried and stomped his foot on the wooden floor of the stage. It made a booming sound that startled them all. 'Constable stop these two fools from hurting themselves.'

Constable Daniels helped them both to their feet. Cecil led Maxwell away sobbing.

'Right then Mr Lightfoot, I am charging you with the murder of James Foley!' the Inspector announced. He read him his rights as Constable Daniels placed him in handcuffs. Lightfoot didn't resist. The look on his face told Susie that even he thought it was a foregone conclusion.

They all watched as Inspector Reynolds and Constable Daniels led a handcuffed Karl Lightfoot out of the theatre room.

'At least they don't have far to go,' Hunter said as he brought everyone a cup of tea.

5

Max was excited to hear Susie and Meg come in through the front door. He had been trying to sleep but was secretly waiting for them both.

They crept in quietly into the Kitchen and made themselves a hot chocolate, and a small plate of scones. With Max in tow they headed to the lounge where Woolsworth had left the fire smoldering making the room nice and cozy.

Sinking into the leather lounge Susie took a long sip of her hot chocolate. Max curled up at her feet and drifted back to sleep.

'Oh my I can't believe what a night we have had then,' Meg said, dipping the end of her scone into her hot chocolate.

'Goodness no,' Susie agreed, 'I am sure it was just an unfortunate accident.'

'Yes but Mr Lightfoot as good as confessed in front of us all!'

'Indeed,' Susie bit into her scone and considered the confession. 'I have to wonder if it wasn't the stress of the moment that caused him to do so.'

Meg nodded in agreement.

Susie and Meg discussed every detail moment by moment as they drank their hot chocolates.

'What about poor Irvine?' Meg asked. It was more a statement than a question.

'Yes he was overly emotional, wasn't he!' Susie agreed.

'Come to think of it, there were a few people who were quite emotional. Especially given he wasn't that well liked.'

'Was he not?' Susie asked with interest.

Meg explained that James Foley was not that well liked amongst the village folk. He had inherited the grand house overlooking the village from his mother though he spent most of his time trying to revive his non existent career in Hollywood.

Rumour had it that he had spent every last dollar living an extravagant lifestyle of a movie star yet earned no money of his own. Mostly the village folks were upset with him because the grand house was going to rack and ruin. He only spent a couple of months in it each year and did not carry out the necessary maintenance on the property.

Not to mention the arrogant manner he conducted himself around the village Meg continued. He wasn't liked much because he treated the town folks with total disdain often calling them peasants.

'Oh I had no idea!' Susie said with curiosity.

'Oh yes he was not liked at all,' Meg carried on.

She told Susie about having demanded a table be made available to him immediately when he went to eat with some Hollywood friends at The Rock Lobster restaurant. At the time the Rock Lobster was the hottest restaurant in all of Cornwall. He hadn't booked ahead, and the place was full. He put on a scene when they refused his demands and he swore to create a volley of bad press for them.

'And what happened?'

'Well I am sure he talked poorly of them around town, but it didn't amount too much.'

Meg added that she wouldn't be surprised if he was murdered. The hard part was going to be finding out who of the many possible suspects would be the one who did it.

'Oh that does sound a challenge!' Susie smiled and finished the last of her hot chocolate.

6

The next morning Susie headed into Polmerton. She had to visit Hunter at the bakery to discuss the next steps they need to take with the Cornwall Cooking School. They had agreed to host a giant tea party at Ash Castle as part of the promotion for the school.

There was lots to discuss as Hunter led Susie out the back to the garden. It was one of Susie's favourite places in Polmerton. Hunter a keen gardener had spent many years developing what he called his private garden oasis. It was tucked in behind the bakery. Across the garden courtyard he had his residence which was converted from old horse stables. The ground was cobbled with old bricks. From every nook and cranny there grew delightful flowers with an array of colour.

Right in the middle of the courtyard a giant oak tree rose up into the heavens. It was buzzing with bird life as they sat down.

Hunter had made them a giant pot of tea that was piping hot. Aimee, his shop assistant, brought out a tray of his jam shortbread tarts. Susie had mentioned to them both previously what a great morning tea treat they made. So at every morning tea party since she was treated to a freshly baked tray.

'Wasn't that a business last night then hey?' Hunter said in his usual jolly manner. Susie had to agree and mentioned it was so unexpected.

Hunter laughed.

'Unexpected that a murder should take place on opening night?' he asked, 'or that James Foley should be the victim?'

'Well, both really!'

'No, no, it didn't surprise me. There was more than one person around town that had it in for him you know.'

'Is that so?' Susie asked in search of more information.

'Oh yes. Many a folk would have done it given half a chance. Not well liked you know.'

Susie watched as Hunter drained his tea and promptly poured himself another.

'Where you surprised it was Karl Lightfoot then?' Susie asked.

'No, not really! The two of them hated each other. Karl always felt that Foley stole the limelight from him. He would have been the leading man if it wasn't for Foley coming back to town each year.'

'So do you think he could have done it then?'

'Well the police seem to think so, and he did confess!'

'Yes but I wonder if that was just the stress of the moment?'

'Could have been I guess. It would have been easy for him to switch out the blanks and add in a real bullet thought wouldn't it?'

Susie explained the conversation she overheard between Constable Daniels and Karl Lightfoot. She recalled that Lightfoot said the gun was lost moments before he was to go on stage. He panicked and at the last moment someone handed the gun to him, but he wasn't sure who it was.

'Well that is interesting then,' Hunter said thinking out loud. Susie paused giving him a moment to gather his thoughts. She could see the cogs of his mind churning over the events of the night.

'What's that dear?' she asked not able to wait any longer.

Hunter told Susie that he was in the kitchen twenty minutes before opening helping Patty out. Cecil Miller arrived in the kitchen and asked me to bring a fresh pot of tea for Irving Maxwell. In his hand he was spinning the prop gun.

He demonstrated the hand actions required to spin a gun like the cowboys would do in an old western movie. The mood was light and everyone was happy. He just seemed to be playing with the gun like a child might do.

About five minutes later he took the pot of tea on a tray up to the back of the stage to the green room out the back. Irvine Maxwell had a few of the actors gathered around and he was talking about the importance of dramatic acting. Don't just hold the gun he said to Lightfoot, thrust it at him in a menacing way.

Hunter left the tray of tea for Mr Maxwell and the last words he heard him say where 'Let's make tonight go off with a BANG!'.

'Oh that is interesting,' Susie responded. She was mentally filing away the information and decided she would visit with Maxwell.

'I didn't make much of it at the time, you know I was busy and all.'

Hunter helped himself to another jam shortbread.

'Well no, you would not have thought much of it. It would have come across as a director giving last minute instructions to his cast.'

'Yes exactly. But I suppose anyone in that room could have switched the bullets if Maxwell had put the gun down.'

Susie pulled a small notebook out of her purse. She had a terrific memory however her dear friend Margery had suggested she might want to take notes of important details.

'So who was in the room, do you recall?' she asked him, pen poised at the ready.

'Oh lets see, there was Irvine Maxwell, Cecil Miller, James of course, and Karl Lightfoot,' Hunter paused to pour Susie more tea.

'And?' she prompted him before he lost his train of thought.

'Oh and, Patty Malone was there along with Janet Brown. She was bent down mending the hem of Karls puffy pirate pants. And young Mandy.'

'Now which one is Mandy again?'

Hunter explained that Mandy was the estranged daughter of James Foley. He told her how she had run away from Polmerton for many years. She didn't have a good relationship with her father but only had to tolerate his presence in the family home for a few months each year.

'Does she work with Patty then?' Susie asked.

'Yes indeed she does.'

7

Susie ended the tea party with Hunter and gave him a hug and a peck on the forehead. He protested briefly that she had cut the meeting short. They hadn't discussed the matter at hand of the cooking school.

She agreed to come back again tomorrow to do so. This delighted Hunter no end as he hoped she would visit every day. She wished Aimee a good day on the way out through the store.

Back on the street she could smell the salty sea air in her nostrils. A gentle sea breeze came up main street from the harbour and wafted around her embracing her. The sun had made an appearance although she assumed it would only be brief judging by the clouds forming out over the seas.

As she walked along Main Street, she glanced in shop windows. Most of the old shops in Polmerton were geared towards the tourist market. Lots of nick knacks and momentos of a holiday in Cornwall. Souvenirs, postcards, and other gift ware items lined the shop windows.

Up ahead she spied Inspector Reynolds. He had a small gathering of towns folks around him all wanting to hear the latest news. Some were concerned there was a killer in their town. Others who had sat in the audience were convinced it was Lightfoot as they saw him pull the trigger that delivered the fatal bullet.

They dispersed as Susie approached.

'Good morning Inspector Reynolds,' Susie greeted him.

'Morning Ma'am!' he nodded.

'I was wondering if I might have a word?' she asked.

'Yes I thought you might want to do so.'

The Inspector led her into the police station. She hadn't been into the station since the messy situation with the Mayor. Then it was a solid mess with piles of paperwork everywhere gathering dust. It was dimly lit, and the curtains had been drawn closed making it a dark and dingy place.

Susie smiled at the difference as she took a seat. Now it was bright, light and clean.

'Young Constable,' the Inspector informed her, 'gave the place a proper clean up then.'

'Oh that is good news,' Susie smiled again.

'Oh aye, it is, but now I can't find anything at all.' He laughed, and he explained that he was sure he was just wanting to impress young Meg. She had taken to popping in on occasion with some home made scones, or some Heva Cake and all.

Susie laughed, 'Good thing as it has a more pleasing atmosphere in here now.'

'Yes, now what can I do for you? I'm rather busy tidying up this mess from last night.'

She nodded and considered that he must have a lot of enquiries to make.

'Paperwork, you know, takes an age.'

'Yes, well Inspector, I wondered how you are getting on with your enquiries into the matter?'

'Enquiries?' he asked confused by the question.

'Yes indeed, interviewing some key players on the night?' she prompted him.

He looked confused. He thrust his hips to the right and the old swivel chair went with him. The file on top of the fresh new pile had the words FOLEY in large black print. The Inspector placed it in front of him on the desk and tapped it with his finger for Susie to see.

'We have all the witness statements in hear Lady Carter,'

'Oh yes I am aware that Constable Daniels took the statements last night, but have you had a chance to dig into them? You know, look a little closer like someone investigating a crime might?' she asked. She wondered if she had pushed the matter a little too far with the inference he wasn't doing a sufficient amount of investigating.

'Well I think we all saw what we saw Lady Carter!'

'True, there were plenty of witnesses indeed,' she had to agree.

'And what we saw was Karl Lightfoot point the gun and pull the trigger, did we not?' he asked. She sensed he was growing impatient with her.

'Yes, we did all see him point the gun from the props department at him. But it doesn't make sense that a gun that only fires blanks all of a sudden now fires a real bullet, does it?'

The Inspector scratched his chin. His right eye drifted towards the clock. It was 12:31 PM so it would soon be lunch. By his calculations he had three years, two months and five days to go until retirement. His mind drifted off to the time when he could be sun baking himself on some remote island of the coast of Thailand.

He didn't respond so Susie continued. She asked him what line of questioning he was following to establish a motive.

'Lady Carter, need I remind you that you are not part of the police force as far as I am aware!' he said tapping his thick long index finger on the file.

She nodded in agreement somewhat reluctantly.

'Yes but,'

'And the man practically confessed to all and sundry shortly after the incident, did he not?' he cut her off from her protest.

'Well yes but,' she tried again to interject.

'And are there not a hundred witnesses who will attest to such?'

'Yes true.' She agreed.

'And everyone saw him pull the trigger!'

'True yes,' she said trying to find the right words to demonstrate to him that perhaps there was more to the case.

'Case closed then Lady Carter!'

'Well what about a motive then?' Susie asked.

He leaned back in the old leather swivel chair. She could see him thinking about how he was best going to deal with the pest in front of him. She imagined he was probably thinking she had watched one-to-many Miss Marple Murder Mysteries on the TV.

'As I said before Lady Carter, we have a hundred witnesses, we all saw him pull the trigger, and he confessed on stage. We don't need a motive as such given all the solid evidence!'

'I see,' she responded.

'Good day to you then Lady Carter,' he said standing up.

Susie felt a little embarrassed that she had poked her nose in and annoyed the Inspector. She stood and offered a brief apology for the interference and left.

She stepped out of the police station door and back onto Main street. Constable Daniels just about walked into her. He was on the return trip from the Famous Polmerton Bakery bringing with him Cornish Pasties and some delights for afternoon tea.

'Good Morning Lady Carter,' he beamed a wide smile pleased to see her.

'Oh Constable Daniels, how wonderful to see you.'

'Oh, that was a sad business last night and all,' he said to her.

'Indeed it was and it must have ruined your date with Meg,' he said.

'Oh Meg,' he smiled, his mind drifted as he thought about her.

Susie asked if he would be coming to visit her tonight to make up for their date being cut short last night. He said he would not as her cousin Emma was visiting.

'Oh you don't say,' Susie responded. Now that he mentioned it she did recall a conversation from last week about Emma coming for tea. Tonight must be the night she thought.

'Yes apparently Emma has recently become engaged and the two of them are going to look at wedding magazines to pick out a dress and all,' he informed her. His cheeks flushed red just a little.

'Oh that is good news,' Susie told him, 'nothing like a good wedding now Constable Daniels, is there?'

'Oh no, we all love a good wedding,'

'And is there a date set?'

'Oh I hadn't given it much thought really,' he responded.

'No I meant for Emma?' she replied.

He told her he wasn't sure but no doubt it would be before the summer was over.

'Sounds like a grand plan, make sure you do give it some thought Constable Daniels,' she smiled at him as she went on her way.

'Oh aye, I certainly will,' he said as she departed.

8

The mood in the Smugglers Inn was sombre. Only a few locals were in for lunch which was probably best Susie felt.

She overheard one old sea dog mention there hadn't been a murder at the Smugglers Inn for a hundred years or more. Back then though they were a lot more frequent. He wondered if they would be returning to the lawless days of the past. Not if Inspector Reynolds had anything to do with it they joked.

Patty Malone was found in the theatre room at the back. She had a cleaning crew in last night to clean the blood off the stage area. Forensics and the police hadn't left until ten pm. Now she was packing away the chairs and tidying up.

'Patty dear how are you feeling?' Susie greeted her with arms out wide.

'Oh, I've had better days for sure,' she replied. She wiped the sweet from her brow with her forearm.

'No doubt indeed,' Susie agreed. 'Just thought I would pop in and see you were making out okay?'

'Oh, so kind of you Susie. Yes I'm okay,' she replied shaking her head. 'It's young Mandy I am worried about.'

Patty explained that with her father now dead she had no one in her life to help her. She was still young at 32 and not very worldly. Patty felt she didn't know how to get on in the world so well. Most importantly though she had no one to lend her emotional support, or even to help her organise the funeral once the body was released from forensics.

Susie nodded her head in agreement as Patty spoke.

She went on and told her of the strained relationship she had with her father and whispered there may have been some money troubles brewing in the background.

At Susie's suggestion Patty wrote down the address for the grand house on the hill. She informed Susie that you couldn't really miss the house as it sat above the village. Susie was sure she had seen it.

'How did the family come by their money then?' Susie asked.

'Shipping company I believe,' Patty replied. 'Apparently the great grandfather owned a small fleet of cargo ships and would regularly run goods down to the Mediterranean and back. A tidy little business that made them moderately wealthy, but most of that money is now gone.'

'Sad to hear,' Susie said.

'Indeed, so if you could drop in and visit her it would be grand. Just to make sure she is okay you know?'

'I shall do so right now Patty, thank you.' Susie said as they hugged goodbye.

Back on the street and in daylight Susie studied the map Patty had drawn for her.

She made her way up the winding streets behind main street. They wound their way up the hill, one tight turn after another. The streets were picture-book perfect lined with rows of quaint little fishing village cottages. Each one no doubt with a story or two to tell Susie thought.

Finally Susie arrive at the address written on the map.

Indeed the house was grand and Susie sensed that in its day it would have been one of the finest homes in all of Cornwall.

Susie stood at the driveway. Large wrought iron gates greeted her with the family crest displayed. The colour on the crest had faded, and a screw had come loose on one side. The right-hand side gate was wedged half open. She stepped over weeds and in through the open gate and looked down the drive.

To the right she could see the town of Polmerton below. Colourful little shops lined main street, and tourists and locals wondered the streets. Small yatch's and fishing boats gently bobbed up and down in the harbour. Further afield she could see the ocean all the way to the horizon.

She gasped for breath at the sheer beauty of it.

Susie made her way down the drive and took in the sight of the old home standing proud on the hill. It was made of giant blocks of sandstone. Her mind briefly drifted to another time when the home was built and tried to imagine them hauling these giant slabs of stone up the hill and position them on the walls.

She knocked on the front door and waited. A short time later the door opened and a sad looking Mandy Reed stood before her.

'Oh Mandy, I've come to check you are okay?' Susie said.

Mandy gave Susie a big hug and asked her in for a cup of tea. She led Susie into the dining room where Susie had a seat. Mandy headed to the kitchen to put the kettle on. She could be heard rattling around in the cupboards.

The lounge room they had just come through and the dining room she now sat in were full of photos of James Foley. Many from his childhood Hollywood star days, and a good number through his young adult life when he was trying to make it as a star. Photos of James with other well known stars and live on stage in theatre productions occupied the best spots on the walls.

'Here we go now,' Mandy said as she returned. She placed the tray of tea and biscuits on the table.

'Now how are you getting on dear?' Susie asked as she poured the tea.

'Oh it was all a bit of a shock really,' she replied.

'Good heavens yes it was, such a terrible business.'

'Not a surprise though. He wasn't much liked around these parts I guess.'

Susie asked her what she meant. Mandy went on to explain because of his nature he was always treating the locals as peasants and that he somehow felt a sense of superiority to them all. This had upset many people in the town.

'Mandy there is something I wanted to ask, but it's a bit delicate,' Susie probed.

'Oh, it's all right Lady Carter. You can ask me anything.'

'Thank you Mandy. Well I was wondering, do you think Karl Lightfoot had reason enough to kill your father?' Susie asked as she took a biscuit.

'Oh, I have been going over that in my mind. It would have been easy enough for him to switch the bullets to real ones I guess,' Mandy replied as she sipped at her tea. 'And there is no doubt he had a rivalry with my dad.'

'Yes,' Susie responded patiently.

'But I don't think he had enough of a reason to do so. I mean, why wait all these years?'

Susie thought about it for a moment. She thought back to the conversation she had with Meg about how this was the seventh year in a row they had run Castaways and the seventh year that Foley and Lightfoot had argued.

'Yes good point dear,'

'I don't really know who did it but I am pretty sure it wasn't Mr Lightfoot.'

'Do you have any thoughts on who might have been responsible?'

'Oh, wait here just a moment,' Mandy said. She walked out of the dining room and shuffled off down a hallway.

Susie looked around the room and was saddened that it was not as fresh as it had once been. Wall paper was peeling off in the corners, and some curtains hung awkwardly from their rods. She had noticed the gardens outside were also in desperate need of attention.

She stood up and walked over to a side table. In the center of the table was a large photo in a frame. The frame had a stand attached at the back. There in the photo was James Foley grinning with his arm around Irvine Maxwell. Maxwell had an equally generous grin. Standing next to them was Cecil Miller who was not grinning.

Mandy walked back in the room with a piece of paper.

'Here,' she said and handed it to Susie. They both took a seat.

Susie looked the paper over. It was an email print out dated from a week ago. The senders email was from a Hotmail account. The tone of the letter was rather threatening.

You have one week to pay up the $300k or else!

'Oh dear,' Susie said and placed the email on the table.

Susie asked her if she had any idea who it might be from.

Mandy shared with Susie that her father had been running out of money for years. He hadn't worked in Hollywood, or anywhere else since his early twenties. So he had spent all of his money inherited from his mother. In a desperate search to make money he had turned to gambling.

'So he owes someone three hundred thousand dollars then?' Susie asked horrified at the thought.

'I guess so. I tried to talk to him about it, but he didn't want to discuss it.'

'Do you know who it was?'

'No idea. Though I think the debt was from the states and not here.'

They both agreed as the email had stated dollars and not pounds it was most likely that it was from someone in the United States.

'Well that would give someone a good reason for murder,' Susie said thinking out loud.

'Yes indeed, and that's not all,' Mandy agreed.

'That's not everything?'

'No, here read this,' Mandy said and handed Susie a hand written note.

It was an IOU hastily written by Foley stating that he owed the sum of fifty thousand pounds to a Mr Irvine Maxwell, dated a year ago.

'Good heavens!' Susie said after reading the note.

'Oh he owed money everywhere.' Mandy said.

9

Meg's cousin Emma had already arrived by the time Susie got back home to the castle.

Max was waiting at the front door for Susie. He had heard the Land Rover making its way up the driveway and came running out of the lounge, took a detour through the kitchen, and up the hallway to the front door.

'Hello Max!' Susie greeted him as she walked up the front steps. He wagged his tail and gave her a bark. She scratched him on the back of the head as she walked through the front doors.

She could hear the squeals of delight coming from the lounge room from Meg and Emma. Susie poked her head in to say hello and wish Emma congratulations on her engagement. Emma was staying for dinner so Susie promised to catch up with them both then.

Upstairs she took a seat on the balcony. She loved the feel of the gentle sea breeze as it rose up the hill and cooled down the castle on a warm day. So much had happened in the last few days her head was spinning. She didn't know what to think of it all.

'Phone Margery!' she said out loud. It's what she had always done since they were teenagers. She and Margery would always talk out their problems and offer a friendly ear mixed with a few words of encouragement.

Margery was delighted to hear from her. The first words out of her mouth were to say how relieved she was that Susie was okay. She had heard about the shooting on the news. It seemed it had received national news coverage with it being a Hollywood star found dead.

'So tell me dear, who do you think did it?' Margery asked.

'I'm not sure at this stage Margery. I'm not convinced it was Mr Lightfoot though all the evidence points to him,' Susie replied.

'Yes I guess there was a hundred or more witnesses who all saw him pull the trigger,' Margery agreed.

Susie said she thought it might have been possible for Lightfoot to have switched out the bullets before the show started, but he had told the Constable the gun was missing prior to the show.

Margery thought about it for a moment. She agreed that it would be the most obvious solution for Lightfoot to do so. But she questioned his motive and Susie had to admit that his motivation was not that strong.

'The thing that worries me,' Margery said, 'Is the sort of gun they have in the props department don't normally fire real bullets.' Margery had spent some time in her twenties acting in the local theatre company in York. Susie would often tell her she should make a comeback as she was quite the dramatic actress.

'Well that is a thought. I guess we will have to wait for the forensics report on the gun to see if it really was the murder weapon.'

They chatted on for a few more minutes. Susie updated Margery about the cooking school and how things were progressing with Hunter. Margery informed Susie she had a new man in her life as well. Fred she had named him. He was a gorgeous little West Highland White Terrier.

Feeling better about life Susie said farewell to Margery with a promise to call again soon. And they both agreed it might be a good idea for Margery to come and visit for a holiday soon.

Susie relaxed for an hour with Max by her side. She tried to doze off but the events of the night before kept occupying her mind.

She showered and dressed before heading downstairs to join Meg and Emma for dinner. Woolsworth preferred a more traditional approach often telling Susie that the help should eat separately.

The three ladies and Max sat down to a fine dinner of roast lamb prepared by Woolsworth. They marvelled at what a great cook he was. Years of practice he had assured them had enabled him to cook at a serviceable level.

'Now Emma, I must hear all about your engagement then,' Susie said. She sipped on her wine as Emma thrust her hand forward to show off her engagement ring. It was a beautifully set half carrat ring that shone in the light.

'How lovely dear,' Susie remarked, 'it seems love is in the air!'. She smiled at Meg as she said it. Meg blushed and tried to hide her face.

'Go on then do tell?' Emma asked.

Meg said she had been on a couple of dates with Constable Daniel. Emma squealed with delight and commented that he was a fine young fellow and very handsome. They all raised a glass to love.

'So what do you think of what happened last night then?' Emma asked them.

'A terrible business,' Meg said shaking her head.

'Such a shock really, to have it happen in front of everyone.' Susie responded.

'Oh I think he will do life for it will Mr Lightfoot!' Emma said making a bold prediction.

'Well, that's if he did it I suppose,' Susie said, 'at this stage we have to wait and see.'

'Oh come on now, everyone saw him do it,' Emma said in disagreement, 'they all saw him pull the trigger. And the gun has his prints all over it.'

They discussed the case further. Susie asked Emma about the procedure that Forensics would go through in such a case. Emma was more than happy to explain it all in detail. The first step would be to recover the bullet from the body. This could then easily be matched to the gun to see if there is a match.

'That will take about three days to get confirmation from the lab,' Emma informed them. 'Once they do, then it will be case closed!'

'Yes I see, but it is possible that someone else switched the bullets before the show without Mr Lightfoot being aware of it, is it not?'

Emma nodded that it was certainly possible but it would be almost impossible to figure out who would do it.

'Unless someone was trying to make Mr Lightfoot look guilty!' Meg suggested.

'Well yes that is an angle I hadn't considered,' Susie said thinking it through.

10

Susie awoke the next morning at around six am. She had a deep sleep and decided she needed to get some exercise to start the day of right.

She called for Max as she put her walking boots on. He was delirious with excitement waving his tail all about. He knew that an early morning walk in the woods behind the castle was awaiting him.

For the next hour they climbed the hill to the highest point. Susie took a seat on a rocky ledge and took in the view across the town of Polmerton and further to the south where she could see a large portion of Cornwall laid out before her.

Susie thought about what Meg had suggested. Was it possible someone else may have switched the bullets in the gun in order to frame Karl Lightfoot. She decided after some consideration it was possible but unlikely. To do so would have meant that an innocent man had to die. She discarded the idea.

'Max!' she called out after about twenty minutes. The wind had got up, and she was starting to feel a chill. Max had been busy. So much to sniff, and rabbits to chase. He nearly didn't hear her call, but he looked up in time to see her disappear around the bend in the path they had come up. He bolted as fast as he could to catch up with her.

She headed back to home for a hearty breakfast before heading into town.

When she and Max arrived in the kitchen Meg was already busy making them scrambled eggs and bacon. The kettle was whistling away in preparation for making coffee. Susie washed up and then they sat down for morning breakfast.

'I'm so excited for Emma getting married and all,' Meg said.

'Yes its grand news,' Susie replied though her mind was elsewhere.

'Oh I wish it where me,' Meg sighed. She dreamed about the perfect wedding day.

'Give it time dear. Most young men need time to pluck up the courage.'

Meg readily agreed and drank her coffee.

Woolsworth appeared wearing overalls, thick gardening gloves, wellington boots and goggles. He informed the ladies it was wood chopping day to which they both had a giggle. A short time later the sounds of straining limbs could be heard and the occasional chop of the axe striking the timber. Max followed him outside and watched from his favourite spot under the oak tree.

Meg noticed Susie was somewhat lost in her own thoughts. 'Something troubling you Susie?'

Susie sighed.

'Oh it's just this whole business with Mr Foley being shot. And now it seems Mr Lightfoot was going to take the blame, regardless.'

'Yes, it does seem likely he did it though, seeing as how we all saw him do it. Don't you think?'

'Well yes, however I am not convinced his motive is strong enough. There may be others with stronger motives.' Susie responded. She shared what she had learned yesterday from Mandy. They talked about the three hundred thousand dollars in gambling debt's and the threatening note. And the fact he owed Irvine Maxwell money as well.

'Oh well fifty thousand pounds is a lot of money,' Meg suggested, 'though I understand Mr Maxwell is loaded with money.'

'Yes but still it does give one a motive,' Susie replied.

Meg thought about it for a moment. She stated that despite the loan of the money she couldn't see him doing it. He appeared to adore Foley, and she did not think he would ever want to harm him. Susie nodded in agreement.

'I might just pop into town and see how the Inspector is getting on with the case,' Susie said and finished the last of her coffee. She had made up her mind that she would not let the Inspector get by without fully investigating the case.

An hour later and Susie pulled her Land Rover into a parking bay a block from the police station.

'Lady Carter. And to what do we owe the pleasure of your company this morning?' Inspector Reynolds sighed as she walked in and took a seat.

Susie inquired as to how the investigation was getting on. The response she received was that there was not much of a need to investigate anything. It was an open-and-closed case as far as he was concerned. The eye witness accounts alone would be sufficient to put Mr Lightfoot away for life.

She pondered for a moment whether to give the Inspector the details about Foley's gambling debts and accounts of money owed to others.

'Inspector, have you asked around to see if others might have had a motive to kill Mr Foley?' she asked.

'Well young Constable Daniels here took all the eye witness accounts. I've been through them indeed. None of them though discount the fact that Lightfoot is as guilty as the night is long!'

Susie smiled and nodded to the Constable who was busy on the phone taking notes as he talked. He smiled back.

'I only ask Inspector as it has come to my attention,' Susie said cautiously, 'that Mr Foley owed considerable amounts of money to various people.'

She informed the inspector of Foley's gambling problems and the enormous sum of money he owed in the US. He took a note as she talked. And she told him about the personal loan from Irvine Maxwell to the sum of fifty thousand dollars.

He wrote the information down and suggested to Susie he would look into it. He took the opportunity to warn her that she was not to be messing in official police business. Susie responded that she would never do such a thing, and she only came by the information when dropping in to enquire about the welfare of young Mandy.

Constable Daniels hung up the phone and said hello to Susie.

'Well then?' the Inspector demanded.

'Right, well that was forensics. They can confirm Mr Foley died of a single fatal gun shot wound to the abdomen region.'

'Yes, yes, we know that part. Get on with it!' the Inspector said growing impatient.

'Well, that is all really, oh, and that Lightfoot's finger prints were all over the gun.' Constable Daniels said pleased with himself for remembering everything.

'Ah, there you go. Finger prints on the murder weapon!' the Inspector said and thumped the table. 'We can close this case here and now then.'

Susie sighed with disbelief. She took a moment to explain to the Inspector that of course his finger prints were on the gun. It was the gun from the play and they had been rehearsing for weeks with Lightfoot handling the gun. Naturally his prints were on it she said with more than a little annoyance.

'Right oh then!' the Inspector responded. He was sure he had other things to do and places to be.

'Oh one other thing,' Constable Daniels said having read his notes, 'Forensics are running some tests on the bullet to see if it is a match for the gun in question. They will know by this afternoon.'

Susie was relieved to hear that forensics were still looking into the matter. She said farewell to them both and headed out into the daylight.

11

The trip out to Marazion took her about twenty minutes. Susie marvelled at the views and the beauty of Mount's Bay. Taking pride of place right there for all to see was the historic St Michaels Mount.

She gasped as she rounded a bend in the road to see the castle on St Michaels Mount rising majestically two hundred and thirty feet above sea level. It was low tide and she could make out people walking along the exposed sand bar.

The coast and its small villages was littered with history. Susie listened fascinated as Patty Malone had shared stories of the notorious pirates and smugglers, the Carter brothers during one of their recent rehearsals. She told the cast that John Carter was named as the 'King of Prussia' as he was from Prussia Cove, and together with his two brothers Harry and Charles, they ran a smuggling operation for many years. Prussia Cove itself was an ideal landing place as it was a sheltered cove with caves. Tunnels led from the caves up to the houses on the hill.

Susie drove through the town of Marazion and took a right-hand turn into Godolphin Place. She made her way up the hill to Godolphin Terrace where she finally found the house she was looking for.

She walked up the steps and admired the beautiful manicured gardens that adorned the property. The house itself was a lovely seaside two level cottage. She turned at the doorstep to take in the view across the bay and breath in the fresh salty air.

The security screen door was unlocked, so she pulled it open and rang the door bell.

A moment later she could hear the patter of little feet coming down the hallway and a few excited barks. This was followed shortly there after by the sounds of human feet.

The door flung open, and she was greeted by Cecil Miller in his navy blue velvet robe with matching slippers. Next to him was Crystal the pure white Labradoodle who was curious as to who the visitor might be.

'Hello Cecil dear, how are you?' she asked.

'Lady Carter how wonderful to see you,' he responded and air kissed her on both sides. 'Do come in.'

Cecil was a handsome and charming fellow Susie had thought. He was in his early forties and kept himself fit and trim running around the hills of Cornwall daily. From a young age he had a love of the theatre after his mother had taken him to see a Shakespeare production of Macbeth for his tenth birthday. He had loved it so much he made up his mind to work in the theatre that night. By the age of 18 he had found the older Irvine Maxwell, and the two were inseparable ever since.

Susie had learned that since moving to Cornwall he had started his own digital media agency working exclusively with theatre production companies.

She followed Cecil and Crystal down the long hallway. Out the back was a lovely modernised kitchen with delightful dining area. It opened up into a conservatory which had generous views of the surrounding gardens.

The dining room had two large mounted trophy deer's heads proudly displayed. Photos adorned the walls of Cecil and Irvine posing with various kills they had succeeded in. A couple of photos looked like they were from Africa, and one or two Susie thought might have been from the Scottish Highlands.

'Irvine and I love hunting. It's the only manly thing we do really,' Cecil explained.

'Oh, I had no idea.' Susie said.

'Well we haven't been for an age. Life has just been too busy, you know how it is.'

Susie nodded.

'So all our hunting gear is in storage sadly.'

Cecil put the kettle on.

'What brings you out here Lady Carter?' he asked as he gathered cups and saucers.

'Oh I was taking in the sights, doing the tourist thing you know. And I suddenly remembered you and Irvine lived out this way.' She explained. 'Thought I would drop in and see how you were both getting on.'

Cecil sighed. His mind reliving the awful incident.

'Yes it was quite a shock really,' he said. 'Poor Irvine has not taken it well.'

'Oh the poor dear I do hope he is all right?'

Tea bags were placed in the tea cups and spoons clattered in the saucepans. Cecil fumbled in an overhead cupboard for a tin of Cornish shortbread. They were his favourite he told Susie, made by the Simply Cornish Biscuit Company.

'He is very upset I'm afraid,' Cecil informed her. 'He hasn't come out of his room since.'

With that he walked up the hallway towards the front door. Crystal was momentarily torn between sniffing further at the visitor or following her master. Following won out.

Susie heard Cecil bang on the door at the front of the house.

'Irvine, love. We have a visitor?'

There was a brief pause before he repeated the routine. A muffled voice in response was all Susie could make out from the kitchen.

Cecil returned and poured the tea into three mugs. He offered Susie milk and sugar.

'It must have been an awful shock for you both?' Susie asked.

'Oh a shock yes, but not really a surprise.' Cecil responded casually without much emotion. She had thought that had she not known about his relationship with Irvine that she would never have known he was gay.

'Not a surprise?' she asked.

'Not really. He was a horrid man, really. Lots of people probably wanted to do him in,' Cecil responded. He took a shortbread and dipped it deep into the tea. It was dangerously deep Susie thought and risked losing a good portion of the biscuit into the cup.

'You don't say?' she encouraged him to continue.

'The only surprise was that it was Lightfoot who did it,' Cecil said. 'I would have done it myself given half a chance.'

Susie sipped her tea and pondered the statement. She wondered if it was a throw away line stated casually over a cup of tea with friends, or if there was any real intent behind it. She decided to try to have him explain further.

'Really Cecil, why would you want to kill Mr Foley?' she encouraged him.

He leaned forward to whisper to her. She put her tea down and leaned in closer to hear what he had to say.

'Not to be blunt but I hated the man!' he stated firmly under his breath.

'Really?'

Cecil went on to explain how Foley was arrogant and rude to him all the time. He treated him as an inconvenience that was always in the way whenever he wanted to talk to Irvine. At one point even going so far as to push him out of the way as he was standing between them.

'Just shoved me out of the way he did,' Cecil laughed reliving the memory. 'I was furious of course but Irvine talked me down.'

Susie nodded her head as she recalled the scene herself. She had thought at the time it was awfully rude of James. As a newcomer to the Castaways crew though she didn't feel it was her place to interfere at the time. Now she was thinking it might have been wise.

'And there was that other matter as well,' He continued.

'Oh, what was that dear?'

'Well Irvine always falls for the stars you know, even though he has me,' Cecil replied. There was a moment of sadness that came across his face.

'How do you mean?'

'Well anyone that has been in Hollywood was a star in his eyes. And he would fall for them each and every time.'

'You don't mean?'

'Oh yes! He and James had quite the affair a few years ago when he was engaged to that Brown woman,' said Cecil. He sipped on his tea and called out for Irving to come and join them. Rustling sounds could be heard up the hallway.

'Oh dear,' responded Susie, 'I don't mean to pry dear but what happened?'

'Irvine had a fling with the Hollywood star. Awfully cliche of him, but he did it just the same.'

'Oh I am sorry to hear that,' Susie said sympathetically.

'It was a brief liaison,' a croaky voice called out from behind them. The sounds of shuffling feet could be heard coming down the hallway.

Irvine Maxwell appeared at last looking a bit the worse for wear Susie thought. At 63 he was in quite good health. He was rake like thin and stood at about five foot eleven inches. Susie had noticed he walked with a slight limp and he appeared disjointed at the wrists. Overtly gay and highly eccentric were part of his endearing nature.

This morning he appeared dishevelled. The few strands of grey hair on his balding head stood to attention as if charged by static electricity. He appeared in his dressing gown and slippers. Crystal had run up the hallway to greet him and had followed him back to the Kitchen.

His eyes were puffy. A tired expression across his face complimenting his slumped shoulders. The look of a man who had the worries of the world on his shoulders at the moment he realises that all hope is lost.

'He was a great actor and highly under rated!' Irvine said as he took a seat and pulled his tea closer. 'Darling how are you?' he asked Susie.

'I am very well thank you Irvine, and you?'

'I've been up all night bawling!'

'Yes! I can't imagine you would cry so much for me when I'm gone,' Cecil said sounding hurt.

'Your not dead honey,' Irvine replied.

'It was a great shock,' Susie added.

For the next few minutes they talked about the tragic events of the night. It took everyone by surprise they all agreed. Irvine and Cecil both made a point of noting that even though it was a shock on the night, they were not at all surprised it happened.

'He was a darling but such a brat,' Irvine said.

'Yes there was something I wanted to ask you about him, if that is okay with you?'

'Oh ask me anything darling, I am a complete open book.'

'Thank you, yes well it's rather awkward really,' responded Susie not sure where to start. She pulled the note out of her handbag that she had been given by Mandy. Folding out the creases she handed it across to Irvine.

'Oh that,' he said after looking at the note.

'Yes, I hope you don't mind me asking. Mandy was concerned about her father having owed money and what the ramifications might be now that he was gone.'

Cecil rolled his eyes in disbelief as Irvine told the story. James had come to visit him about a year ago after the opening night. He said he needed to go over some lines in the play but he knew differently. Foley never questioned the script.

Irvine explained how he came over with a look of desperation on his face. He had run out of money and had debts mounting. Apparently he owed money everywhere. At first Irvine had said no to the request, but he literally begged him and said his life depended on it.

'So I gave in and gave him fifty thousand pounds as a loan,' Irvine explained.

'Yes knowing full well we would never see it again!' Cecil objected.

'He told me he was selling the house and would pay me back in a few months!' Irvine shot back at Cecil with a look of anger. It was clear the discussion had been had a few times previously.

'We will never get the money back now that is for sure!' Cecil said. He stood up from the table and went into the kitchen to fill the jug. The sound of running water was shortly replaced with the sounds of the kettle being plugged in and slowly coming to life.

'Irvine, do you know of anyone else who Mr Foley may have owed money to?' asked Susie.

He thought about it for a moment. Then he shook his head no. He couldn't think of anyone specifically even though Foley had told him of his money troubles previously. It was obvious though he felt that if he had come to him for money, he no doubt went to others.

Cecil was making a noise in the kitchen to Irvine's dismay. He shouted at him to quieten things down as he rubbed at his forehead.

'I must head off Irvine but before I go, do you know of anyone else who might have wanted to harm Mr Foley, or even kill him?' Susie asked.

'What? You mean you don't think Karl did it then?'

'Of course it looks that way at first glance,' responded Susie.

'Everyone saw what happened?' Irvine said in a tone that made it more a question than a statement.

'Smoking gun!' Cecil said popping his head around the corner.

'Yes you are quite right,' Susie said gathering her bag and keys to make her departure. She suddenly felt bad for snooping around and asking questions.

'Unless it was that wretched woman he left at the altar,' Irvine said thinking it over.

Suddenly a loud banging sound could be heard from the kitchen. Cecil screamed and grabbed at the bench top before collapsing with a sickening thud to the floor. In his downward motion he had grabbed out for something solid to break his fall only to latch on to the pots and pans from last nights dinner. They came crashing down on top of him.

Irvine and Susie leapt to their feet and ran into the kitchen.

Cecil was rolling around on the floor in agony holding his left wrist with his right hand. A five inch gash across the palm of his left hand was gushing blood.

Susie grabbed a tea towel and pressed it down hard on the wound.

Eventually Irvine was able to calm him down enough to get him back to his feet. His face was white. On seeing the blood on the floor he momentarily fainted. Irvine slapped him on the face a couple of times to bring him back.

'He's going to need to go straight to the doctors.' Susie said. By the look of the cut he was going to need stitches.

12

Susie helped Irvine bring Cecil to the doctors office in Polmerton. Fortunately, they were able to see him straight away. After cleaning the wound the doctor used five stitches to close the wound.

Cecil squeezed Irvine's hand with his good hand the whole time.

Once she was satisfied everything was okay Susie bid them farewell and walked into town. She passed by the usually quiet post office and Natwest bank. On passing she was shocked to hear a commotion happening inside the bank. She paused for a moment to listen. There was a que, so she was unable to make out what was happening. At best she was able to figure out that some woman wanted her money returned, and she was very angry about it.

She checked her watch. It was 3.15 pm. Goodness she thought to herself. She was tied up in the doctors quite a bit longer than she had thought. For a moment she debated if it was too early for her to return to the police station. She ran the risk of annoying the Inspector which she didn't want to do. On the other hand, Constable Daniels had said that further test results were due back this afternoon from the forensics team.

The police station was only a block away. She decided to drop in and just see what the update was. Along the way she stopped to chat with some locals whose faces had started to become familiar to her.

As she passed Hunters shop, the 'Famous Polmerton Bakery', she noticed something rather peculiar. A large black Ford Kuga with tinted windows pulled up outside the police station. The door to the police station opened and out came Karl Lightfoot with a rather serious looking man in a tailored suit. She watched in disbelief as they got into the Ford Kuga, and the driver sped away.

'Good heavens!' she said out loud to no one and picked up her pace to the police station.

On her arrival she pushed the large wooden door open, ducked her head, and walked inside.

'Hello Inspector, Constable,' she said nodding to them. The faster pace had led her to lose her breath. She took a seat and composed herself.

'Well it doesn't take long for word to get about, does it now?' the Inspector enquired. He didn't sound pleased. In fact he sounded downright upset Susie felt. And rightly so. The number one suspect, a man everyone in town automatically assumed was guilty, just walked out the door.

'Oh, I have heard nothing,' she assured him. 'I was just walking past when Mr Lightfoot emerged into the light on foot?'

'I see,' the Inspector said and placed some paperwork into the Foley folder.

'What on earth happened?' Susie asked.

'Forensics!' Constable Daniel answered.

'Oh?'

'Yes it appears the bullet that killed Mr Foley could not have come from the gun used in the performance.' The Inspector reluctantly informed Susie.

'You don't say?' Susie said prompting them to reveal more.

'So it couldn't have been Mr Lightfoot who killed him,' Daniels filled in the missing information. He beamed from ear to ear. Susie sensed he had a real passion for crime work and she figured he might one day make a good detective.

'At least that is what his lawyer argued just now,' the Inspector said. He stood up and placed the file on top of the filing cabinet. A makeshift kitchen bench in the back corner housed the kettle. He walked over and flicked the switch as he asked Susie what she would like. She responded with her usual.

'There must have been a second gun then?' Susie asked hoping they were already working on finding the second shooter.

'Now now, this is not the grassy knoll, or downtown Dallas. This is Polmerton and we have none of that here.' The inspector didn't want to cause a panic among the town folks by letting out that there was a second shooter on the loose.

Constable Daniels was reading the print out of the forensics report.

'May I?' she asked him with hand outstretched.

'Oh. Agh, okay.' He said and handed it to her.

Susie read through the detailed analysis of the bullet that had been extracted from Foley. She skipped past the technical data and went straight to the conclusion. It stated that the bullet was most likely to have come from a hunting rifle such as the Remington 700.

Her mind flashed back to the gun cabinet her Uncle Charles had at the castle. Woolsworth, the butler, had tried to show her the collection about a week after she had moved in. Not being that interested in guns she declined the invitation to inspect them.

The Inspector returned with three mugs of tea, and a plate of jam shortbread biscuits. He placed them on his desk and took a seat. Susie followed his lead.

'These look nice,' she smiled at him. She was tempted to tease the Inspector as to the origins of the biscuits but she thought better of it judging his mood today.

'Oh yes they are freshly baked today by Mr McGill!' Constable Daniels answered as he took one and dipped it into his tea.

Susie handed the Inspector the forensics report. She informed him that she was no expert in guns and the like, but at least now they had something solid to go on. Now we know what we were looking for at the very least.

The Inspector took the opportunity to remind her that she was not part of the investigation, and that there was no 'we' as far as it went. Naturally she nodded in agreement and determined to ignore his concerns.

'Yes of course Inspector,' she smiled at him, 'however I was wondering if we shouldn't start the investigation by taking a closer look at the scene of the crime. Maybe there are some clues we overlooked.'

The Inspector discussed the idea with Susie for a moment. He informed her that he had an appointment for most of the afternoon investigating a burglary. Mrs Harrow, an old friend of his mothers, had some missing items out of her garden shed. As much as he wanted to investigate the shooting incident further his priorities were elsewhere.

'Oh that's a shame!' she replied, 'What about Constable Daniels here?'

'The lad has to track down a flock of sheep gone missing, from the Johnston's farm out on Faulthead Road, first.' The Inspector replied. 'After that he can focus his attentions on the shooting incident.'

Constable Daniels took his cue to leave. On the way out the door he shared with Susie how the Johnstons had been calling all morning about twenty missing sheep. He felt it was best he went and sorted that first so he would have a clear mind to look deeper into the death of Mr Foley.

Deciding she was going to have to go it alone Susie bid them both good day and headed out the door after Constable Daniels.

She watched as Daniels hopped in the station police van and headed off to find the missing sheep. Having met the Johnstons Susie was sure they probably just forgot which paddock they had penned them in.

13

Susie turned around and saw Meg come out of the Famous Polmerton Bakery with a load of goodies.

'Good heavens, what have you got there?' Susie enquired.

Meg reminded Susie that the Aunties were coming for dinner tonight. She had taken the liberty of getting some desert. She had a lovely sponge cake, scones, and of course Susie's favourite, the jam tart shortbreads.

Susie had completely forgotten about the prior engagement. Originally it had been booked as a celebration and reflection of the success of the Castaways play. Now it was more likely to be a post-mortem of the night. Regardless they were good company and Susie always enjoyed their cheerful banter.

They chatted on the street for a moment. Susie informed Meg that she was about to go and investigate the scene of the crime more thoroughly. She suggested in the chaos of the night things could have been overlooked. Meg readily agreed to come along and help. They walked to her car together and deposited the goodies inside before heading across the road to the Smugglers Inn.

Patty Malone greeted them with a hearty welcome. There were hugs all round. She seemed glad to see them both Susie thought. Most likely no one had been to see her since the incident happened, Susie thought.

'Oh, you just missed Janet Brown,' Patty informed them. 'She dropped by to see how I was getting on.'

She took two pints of ale to a table in the corner. The gentlemen sitting at the table looked totally out of place in the Smugglers Inn. They had too much style with their dress, and the thick American accents gave them away.

'Tourists!' Patty joked when she rejoined them.

Susie explained why they had popped in, besides wanting to see how she was.

A short moment later and Patty had led them out the back to the theatre room. A professional cleaning crew had been in and totally cleaned the stage area. Patty wanted to have it cleaned as soon as she could she explained to them.

'Well, I will leave you both to have a nosey around then,' Patty said. She had to tend the bar so was not able to join them in the search for clues.

Susie and Meg stood in the now empty theatre room and thought back to the night of the opening of Castaways. Meg commented that it was funny how one minute everyone was happy and singing along, and the next everything changed. Susie reminded her that life could be that way. One minute you're flying high, and the next minute your world can come crushing down.

'Where should we start?' Meg asked.

'This way,' Susie said. She walked across the empty room to the side of the stage. She marched up the eight wooden steps that led up to the side of the stage and stood with her hands on her hips. For a moment she stood there in silence as she surveyed the scene. Meg stood beside her in silence as well.

The moment was broken by the sound of a familiar voice.

'Hello, hello, am I too late?' asked Constable Daniels.

Both Meg and Susie swung around to see the young Constable walking across the empty room and up the stairs.

'Constable Daniels, so glad you could join us so soon!' Susie said.

'Constable,' Meg said shyly.

'Yes well it turned out the Johnston's had forgotten where they had put their sheep. Found them as soon as I drove up their driveway Lady Carter,' Daniels replied, 'Hi Meg.'

Susie said she was very glad that he could join them. She said what they needed to do was reenact the scene. She directed Daniels to take up the position that James Foley was in moments before he was shot.

He had Meg take the same position as the intruding pirate played by Karl Lightfoot.

Meg tried to act menacing as though she had a gun in her hand and was threatening the young Constable. The problem was Susie chuckled to herself, she was beaming from ear to ear at him.

'Right now, if it wasn't the gun in Lightfoot's hand then it was a second shooter,' Susie said thinking out loud. She moved around to the side of the stage and raised her hands into the position one would take if they had a rifle in their hands.

The general conclusion was that there was more than enough space to the side of the stage for the culprit to stand and get a clear shot at Foley. All he had to do was wait for the right moment, and when Lightfoot went to pull the trigger on the prop gun, fire at the same time.

Susie concluded that in the commotion that followed the gun might have been easily hidden somewhere. In fact it was probably still here backstage.

The three of them spent the next thirty minutes searching every nook and cranny they could find but came up short.

They took a seat on the steps to gather their thoughts.

'Is it possible that someone brought the rifle in with them on the night and then took it away again?' Meg asked.

'Oh yes, I think so!' Constable Daniels replied happily.

'Yes I suppose it would be possible,' Susie agreed, 'but how would they get it in here, and then out again without anyone noticing?'

They discussed different ideas on how someone might bring in a fully loaded rifle unnoticed, shoot dead the leading actor, and then leave with the rifle again unnoticed. It seemed highly unlikely they all agreed. Probably too much of a risk as well.

'Let's do another search in case we missed something,' Susie said.

They all got up and started a new search. Meg and Daniels searched the stage area while Susie went backstage into the room where the actors would gather and prepare.

In one corner of the room was the costumes department. Janet Brown had down a great job with the costumes this year. She had set up a rack for the costumes to hang from. She also had a small table with a sewing machine and other sewing equipment. A number of large rolls of material where leaning in the corner.

Susie made a mental note to call in on Janet Brown. The poor girl seemed rather distraught when the dreadful incident occurred. She wondered if anyone had thought to check on her welfare at all.

In the other corner of the room was a small desk and two chairs. This was what Irvine had lovingly referred to as his office. He and Cecil would sit there and work on the script and production.

Under the desk was a metal trap door about one a half meters wide and deep. She moved the desk to one side and tried to pull up the metal door. With all her might she pulled against it and finally managed to pull it open.

'That's where they throw the bodies,' came a hearty laugh from behind here.

Susie screamed from shock and dropped the metal door with a thud that echoed around the stage area. Meg and the Constable came running. Susie swung around to see Patty Malone standing next to her grinning.

'Oh dear you have me a fright!'

'Oh, sorry love, didn't mean to!' Patty Malone replied.

'I assume that's a cellar or something?' Susie asked regaining her composure.

'I believe so yes. I've not been game to go down there myself.'

'No I don't blame you!'

'Not been used in the time I have been here. My Dad used to say it was where the smugglers would store all of their loot. Some old locals claim there was once a smugglers tunnel from the harbor to in there!' Patty told them.

'Maybe we should check it out?' Meg suggested.

Patty said she had torches, but it was agreed that only Constable Daniels should go. It was, after all, official police business and part of the investigation. Reluctantly he agreed to go down and take a look.

A few moments later Patty emerged with a torch for him.

Susie and Meg held open the metal door while Daniels made his way cautiously down the wooden ladder into the depths of the cellar. His feet touched the ground with a dull muted thud.

He flashed the torch around and called out that it didn't look like anyone had been down there for many years. There was old furniture piled up gathering mounds of dust. Cobwebs woven optimistically years ago all intertwined.

Daniels found a bricked archway. He shone the torch into it and decided it looked safe enough to enter. Susie and Meg watched as the light of the torch disappeared.

'Be careful!' Meg shouted out after him. They could hear muted sounds of footsteps and furniture being moved around.

They waited patiently for a few minutes. Then the light of the torch came back. Dimly at first but then shortly after it filled the cellar below them. It was followed by the Constable with cobwebs all over the back of his head. His uniform was dusty and damp.

'Are you okay?' Meg asked as they helped him back up the ladder.

Susie let the cellar door back down.

'Well?' she asked impatiently.

Daniels explained that he went through the brick archway. It led into a hallway made of brick. He told them he could tell the place was really old by the style of the brick and the way they were laid.

Once he went through the hallway, it opened up into a cellar. There is even some old bottles of wine down there he said with a smile.

At one end of the cellar there was what looked like it could have been a tunnel. But as he explained it was boarded up. As Patty had said, it didn't look like anyone had been down there in a very long time.

'So brave,' Meg sighed. She started to brush the dust of his shoulders and pull the cobwebs out of his hair.

'No sign of the rifle then?' Susie asked as she watched Meg fuss over him.

'No nothing sorry. If there was a rifle, then it's not down there.'

14

The Aunties arrived promptly at five thirty pm dressed in their finest dining dresses. They made a point about being on time for social occasions. In fact, they had built a good deal of their reputation about town on the back of their promptness.

Attention to detail was the other thing they were well known for. They were often heard to say that attention to detail was of the utmost importance. If you are going to host a tea party, then for heaven's sake, do it properly.

Mildred and Mable Milford were twin sisters born and bred in Polmerton. They were both engaged to handsome young men many years ago, but sadly both were killed in the war. So they determined that they would make a life of being local celebrities instead. Susie had been informed that they were perhaps the best informed and connected people in the whole district. Towns folk would often look to them for the latest news around town, and their seal of approval could make or break a person on the social calendar.

Susie had led them into the lounge room where Woolsworth had prepared a fire. It was crackling away as they sat down in the plush leather lounge chairs. A bottle of red from the main land was produced and four glasses poured.

'Where is young Meg?' Mildred asked.

Susie explained she was on the phone to her new love.

'Oh yes Constable Daniels, a fine young fellow!' Mable said.

'What a handsome couple they make,' Mildred added.

A few moments later Meg joined them sitting next to Susie on the opposite couch. Susie handed her a glass of wine and they toasted the night ahead. Naturally the Aunties quizzed Meg on her blossoming relationship. Meg's face flushed red, but she had to admit she was quite keen on the Constable.

'Oh by the way, I have something I need to return,' Mildred said. She had been carrying a bag with her which Susie had thought looked rather heavy for her.

Susie watched as Mildred opened the bag and pulled out a pile of books. They were mostly older books and there was at least fifteen of them. Mildred explained that she had borrowed them from Charles a few years ago and hadn't got around to returning them. She decided now was an opportune time to do so.

'There is one or two in there you might find interesting dear,' Mabel said.

Susie flicked through the pile of books and was intrigued by some titles. There was 'A Brief History of Cornwall', 'Tin Mines In Cornwall', and 'The Unofficial History of Polmerton' written by Charles Ash III himself. It was the last one that got her interest though. It was 'A Smugglers Guide To Cornwall' which she promised herself to read in the next few days. She seemed to recall seeing the book somewhere but for the moment, with all the excitement of the day, she couldn't recall where.

Woolsworth rang the bell indicating dinner was ready.

They followed Susie into the dining room and found their places. More wine was poured as he served them freshly made pumpkin soup. Susie informing the Aunties that Woolsworth had grown the pumpkins himself.

'Now about that business the other night,' Mildred started to say.

'Oh it was a messy turn of events,' Mabel interrupted.

'Yes, very messy,' Mildred had to agree. 'Do you know if they have much to go on? I hear that Mr Lightfoot is off the hook?'

Susie finished her soup. She marvelled at their ability to be on top of the town gossip. She explained that at this stage there are a number of suspects who had a reason to do it but none as strong as Lightfoot appeared to be.

'The real problem right now is figuring out what happened. The bullet came from a rifle but no rifle was found at the scene. And then there is the business of being able to get the rifle into the theatre, and back out again, without being detected.'

The Aunties nodded in unison. They were eager to hear more.

'So it was a rifle then?' Mildred asked.

'Do they know what kind?' Mabel added.

'Most likely a hunting rifle of some sort,' Mildred answered Mabel who agreed with her assessment.

'Yes the report back from the forensics team has suggested a hunting rifle.' Susie confirmed.

Mabel put her spoon down and announced she had it. She knew exactly what they needed to do to solve the crime. Everyone listened with great interest. She explained that all they had to do was go around to every home and find all those who owned a rifle that matched the description. Then the guilty party would feel so bad about what they had done that they would have to confess right away.

Mildred nodded adding it sounded like a sound plan.

'What if they disposed of the rifle though?' Meg asked.

A light bulb went on in Susie's head. If she could just work out where the best place to dispose of a rifle is she might be able to find the murder weapon.

15

After a solid sleep Susie was up early. She had dressed in her gardening clothes and headed out to the garden shed. Max had followed along. He carried with him an old tennis ball Meg had found for him.

He dropped it on the ground in front of him and waited patiently for it to be tossed.

Susie found her small hand shovel, and a bag of fertiliser, and carried both of to the garden bed where she was planting roses. They were James Galway creeping roses by David Austen roses. Her favourites.

She was hoping she could train them to grow up the side of the new arch way she had installed. The path that wound its way down to the rotunda where she like to have morning tea was looking a little bare she had told Woolsworth. He was good enough when he was next in town to purchase two metal arches which he set up about six feet apart. Across the top he secured three planks of wood, and over that some wire mesh.

With the arch way now constructed by Woolsworth, Susie turned her attention to planting out the David Austen creeping roses. She planted several at each end of the two arches. A selection of both white, and pinks with red.

Max watched as she laboured away digging holes and adding fertilizer to them before she upturned the small pots containing the roses. She placed each rose carefully into their new home in the soil and pushed the exposed soil back in and around the rose.

She was on the fourth one when Woolsworth approached her from behind. He cleared his throat to get her attention. Susie was lost in her own world.

'Excuse me Ma'am,' he said.

'Oh, yes Woolsworth, what do you think?'

'Looking lovely Ma'am,' he replied. She almost detected a smile.

'Is it morning tea already?'

Susie took her gloves of. She was quite pleased with the work she done so far this morning. It pleased her to get a bit of gardening done first thing in the morning. Often, she would inform Meg, that it was the key to the good life, just do a little each day consistently. Over time it all added up to a jolly good effort.

'No Ma'am, you have a visitor,' Woolsworth informed her, 'she seems rather distraught!'

'Good heavens,' Susie said getting herself to her feet. 'Who on earth is it?'

'It's Mandy Reed Ma'am,' Woolsworth had turned and was walking away when he added, 'She seems rather upset. I shall prepare morning tea!'

Susie smiled. When she first arrived at Ash Castle, she was worried he wasn't going to accept her as the new owner. Over time though his grumpy manner had turned more pleasant and obliging. Now they got on quite well and often enjoyed a good laugh. He was still very traditional though in many ways.

Returning her things to the garden shed she tried to think what might have upset Mandy enough for her to come out to see her.

She washed up in the laundry and checked her hair in the mirror. Max followed her around as she progressed her way through the laundry, down the hall past the kitchen, into the entrance hall, and across into the lounge room.

Stepping into the lounge room she found Mandy sitting on a lounge with Meg next to her rubbing her on the shoulder. Mandy had been crying clearly. She had a bunch of soggy tissues balled up in her hand. Her eyes were puffy and red, and tears had been streaming down the side of her face.

'Mandy dear, are you okay?' Susie asked rushing over to her.

Many stood up and embraced Susie with a firm hug. She sobbed as she held on to Susie and for a brief moment Susie was not sure she would let go. Eventually she released her grip and sat back down next to Meg. Meg put her arm around her and pulled her close.

'She's had a bit of a fright I'm afraid,' Meg explained. Susie took a seat on the opposite couch. Confused by what was going on, Max walked up to Mandy and put his head on her knee. He looked up at her with his big brown eyes.

'Oh no, what's the trouble dear?'

Mandy choked back tears as she reminded Susie about the threatening email from the Americans claiming she had one week to pay the debt of three hundred thousand dollars. Susie said she remembered the email.

'Well I have had another one,' Mandy said. She reached into her pocket and found the folded up email she had printed out. Leaning over the coffee table separating the two lounge chairs, she handed it to Susie.

Susie unfolded it and read it.

We know your old man is dead but we still aim to collect. Pay up or else!

She placed the email print out on the coffee table and tried to remain calm.

'Oh dear,' Susie said after a brief pause. 'When did this arrive?'

'Yesterday! I didn't want to bother you with it though.' Mandy replied.

'It's perfectly fine dear you can call on us any time.'

'Yes any time at all,' Meg agreed.

'I would have ignored it but then this morning I received a phone call,' Mandy sobbed.

'Oh no?'

'It was an American voice, but there was no international dial tone.'

Mandy explained that whenever her father would call her from Los Angeles, she would always hear the three little beeps as the call connected. In this case though she didn't hear them. It sounded like they were around the corner.

'Now Mandy dear, we don't really know where the call came from,' Susie said trying to reassure her.

'I tried to tell myself that as well. But then I looked out the window earlier and there was a strange car parked at the top of my driveway for a few minutes. There were two men in the car.'

'Oh goodness, and what happened.'

'Some neighbours came by walking their dogs. Well they drove off so I think it might have scared them away for the moment.'

Susie was alarmed by this turn of events but she didn't want that to register on her face. The most important thing right now was to keep Mandy safe and out of harms way.

'Did you notice if you were followed when you left the house?'

'No I wasn't. I kept checking in the rear view mirror but no one followed me here.'

It was clear to Susie that if she wasn't followed to the castle that it was going to be best for Mandy to stay with them until the matter was sorted out. It was one thing for James Foley to have racked up gambling debts, but she didn't think young Mandy should have to suffer as a result. Poor girl had been through enough in her life Susie thought.

'Right here is what we will do,' Susie said, 'Meg will call the police and have them come here to take a statement from you. They can then investigate.'

Meg nodded in agreement. Susie noticed the smile as she thought about spending more time with Constable Daniels.

'And Mandy, you will stay here with us until these two are caught. I don't care how long it takes,' Susie said.

'Oh no, I couldn't do that, are you sure?' Mandy asked.

'Quite sure dear, your safety is most important!'

16

Inspector Reynolds and Constable Daniels arrived about forty minutes later. They had both been tied up with paperwork and seemed pleased for the opportunity to get out and do some real police work.

Woolsworth led them into the lounge room. He had just prepared morning tea for the ladies and offered them the same. They readily agreed. A short while later he returned from the kitchen with additional teacups, saucers and teaspoons.

Meg poured their tea for them and handed one to the Inspector. She picked up the other and walked around to where Constable Daniels. 'Here you are Constable,' she smiled as she handed it to him. Constable Daniels face went bright red as he took the tea from her. He thanked her rather nervously as the others all watched on.

It made Susie feel good to know that despite all the drama that had taken place in the last few days that young love still had a chance to blossom. If only she could figure out how to encourage the young Constable to blossom a bit faster.

'Right oh then,' said the Inspector through sips of his tea. He was not one to make small talk when there was a serious matter for the police to investigate and he was keen to get to it. 'What seems to be the problem then?'

Susie took the lead to explain the initial conversation she had with Mandy and the first email. The Inspector nodded and dunked a shortbread into his tea. She went on to inform them that she was doing a spot of gardening when Woolsworth came to collect her.

On coming inside she found the distraught Mandy being comforted by Meg.

In detail she went over the account given by Mandy and handed across the second email. Mandy sat silently next to Meg who clutched her hand to give her strength. Susie sensed she was feeling more at ease now that the police were here.

'Is that right Mandy? Did I leave anything out?' Susie asked her.

Mandy agreed that she had covered everything. The Inspector asked for more details about the two men sitting in the car. Fortunately Mandy, who had a good eye for art and could draw a reasonably good portrait, was able to give them a reasonably detailed description.

She pointed out that they appeared well dressed, possibly overdressed and that they should stand out if seen in the area. They looked to have been of European descent, possibly Italian or Spanish, and both had darker features. One looked about ten years older than the other. She guessed he was probably in his early forties though he did look fit like he worked out at the gym. He had a tattoo on the side of his neck that looked like an eagle trying to fly out of his collar. The other younger man was leaner with a marathon runners physique. He was the driver of the car. The car itself was a standard issue Hyundai I30 with a Hertz sticker on the back window.

Constable Daniels took endless notes trying to keep up with her as she spoke. Susie watched him as he listened carefully and wrote everything down. A fine young man she thought to herself.

'Right oh then, here is what we will do,' the Inspector said when he was confident he had enough information. 'The young lad here will head into town and ask all the town shop keepers if they have seen these two. If they have been in town, we will soon know it!'

'Start with Patty Malone,' Susie suggested. It just occurred to her that when she visited with Meg yesterday, there were a number of American tourists in the Inn for lunch.

She explained to the Inspector that she seemed to recall seeing them at the Smugglers Inn.

'Returning to the scene of the crime then, they always do!' Constable Daniels added.

'What's that lad? Have you been reading them Murder Mystery novels again?' joked the Inspector.

Daniels laughed it off then continued, 'No, but I mean, if they had been trying to collect money from Mr Foley and he wouldn't pay, then maybe they were responsible for shooting him!'

Susie thought about it and it was as good of an idea as any they had to go on.

'They say that killers always return to the scene of the crime, they can't help themselves!' the Constable added.

'Only in the movies lad!' the Inspector replied. He had pointed out to the young Constable on more than one occasion that they had to work on the facts of a case, and not silly ideas or myths about police work one might read in an Agatha Christie novel.

'Well it's certainly an idea worth pursuing Inspector,' Susie jumped to his defence, 'as we don't have much else to go on in the murder investigation.'

'We are following a number of leads up,' the Inspector informed her.

'Oh that is good to hear, what are the leads?' Susie asked putting him on the spot.

'Well this one for a start!' he replied. The Inspector was starting to get a little flustered. In the end he agreed that given the threats made to Mandy, the two American tourists were the strongest lead they had to work on right now.

17

The next morning Susie decided to have breakfast outside in the rotunda. It was a beautiful morning with the sun trying to break through some low-lying clouds. She was confident it would though she rugged up in her wooly cardigan just the same.

Max sat with her and had a sleep. He had completed his morning routine of sniffing all the garden beds, doing a lap of the lawn area which was quite large. Several times he circled back to the rotunda to check on Susie. He finally did several laps of the old oak tree before returning to the rotunda for the final time. An exciting mornings work and now a sleep was in order. So he plonked himself down and rested his snout on Susie's foot.

Woolsworth had brought her some hard-boiled eggs with wholegrain toast. It was cut into fingers just the way she liked them. She dunked each one in turn into the runny oak. A large pot of tea was produced and Woolsworth had poured her a cup before he returned to his chores in the kitchen.

She read one of the books Mildred had returned, 'A Smugglers Guide to Cornwall.'

It was a fascinating read she thought. The history of smugglers on the Cornwall peninsula was amazing and captivating. The area was littered with little coves and harbours. In the dead of night smugglers would come ashore in tiny row boats. They were laden with illicit goods such as tobacco, brandy and gin. She read with fascination that local Tin Miners, who couldn't work in summer due to lack of water, would turn to smuggling to substitute their income.

Many of the old pubs, warehouses and in fact houses, had tunnels that ran from caves dotted along the coast line. In some cases, vast networks of tunnels would connect numerous buildings and dwellings.

She read with interest that the primary reason for the smuggling was to avoid having to pay the Kings taxes on their goods. As a result some smugglers in the Cornish region had become quite wealthy.

Susie took another cup of tea and thought about it for a moment before her thoughts turned to Mandy. The poor girl had been through a lot in her life Susie thought. Now this business with the threats to pay her fathers debts was really too much.

She made up her mind that Mandy could stay as long as needed to. It seemed that her and Meg were getting along famously. She had heard them giggling like two school girls in the kitchen earlier. It was good for Meg to make some new friends as well. As much as she loved the company of Meg, she was mindful that it was important she spends time with people her own age as well.

The business with these two Americans had her concerned as well. With a bit of luck the Inspector and Constable will be able to locate them soon enough, and things could get back to normal.

She hoped that it happened soon.

Three hundred thousand dollars in debt was a huge amount. She reasoned that Mr Foley must have been desperate indeed to have mounted such a high debt. Like most gambling addicts, he probably had some wins but then chased after his losses as well, she thought.

Her mind drifted towards the day ahead.

She had planned to have a quiet day today. There was some work to do for the next class of the Cornwall Cooking School, which she could do later. Hunter wasn't expecting it until later in the week, anyway.

Instead, she thought she might visit Irvine and Cecil again. Hopefully they might know something about the debt Mr Foley owed to the Americans. Or at the very least, have some contacts in the United States, that may have had contact with Mr Foley.

She went and changed into something more suited to visiting friends. She chose a nice pair of navy slacks, and a peach blouse.

Over the top she pulled her full length overcoat just in case she needed it.

Before long she was on her way to Marazion.

Susie marvelled at the sites as she came around sweeping corners offering views across the water. She loved the rugged coastline and wondered why it took her so long to come back to Cornwall.

Finally she made it to the home of Irvine and Cecil. Earlier she had phoned ahead to see if they would be available for a morning tea. Naturally they readily agreed hoping there would be plenty of gossip.

After a big greeting at the front door, Susie followed them down the hall to the dining area. She took a seat while Cecil fixed tea in the kitchen. Crystal the dog could smell Max on her. She sniffed up and down Susie's leg and decided she was okay.

'Wonderful to see you again Susie,' Irvine said as he took a seat.

'Thank you, and you too.'

She enquired as to how Cecil's wounded hand was getting on. He showed her the stitches, and she agreed with him that it was healing nicely.

'So tell us everything, how is the investigation going?' he asked. Irvine polished his glasses with a tissue while he listened.

Susie updated them on the fact that Karl Lightfoot had been released from custody. She told them about the forensics report which clearly showed that the prop gun in the play was not the one that fired the bullet.

'I thought as much,' Cecil called out from the kitchen, 'it seemed like the prop gun was so old that the right bullets wouldn't be available to buy!'

'At least not easy to find,' Irvine added. 'You would probably need a specialist gun dealer who dealt in antiques and such.'

Susie agreed with them.

Cecil brought a tray with a large pot of tea. He had broken out their finest tea set with matching cups and saucers. Susie commented how lovely it looked. Cecil told her that Irvine had brought the set for his birthday knowing how much he liked a good tea party.

'It did look like he had done it though didn't it?' asked Cecil as he took a seat. He poured tea for the three of them and handed Susie a cup.

'Oh yes it did. Everyone was so convinced it was him simply because it looked that way!' Susie agreed.

'Well that's often the way it goes,' said Irvine. 'Looks can be deceiving.'

'True, they can.'

Cecil asked who the police were focused on as far as a main suspect was concerned with this new evidence. He fed Crystal shortbread biscuits under the table.

Susie explained that this was partly why she had come to visit them. There were no really solid leads at this stage. There were a number of people who had reason enough to do it, but no solid evidence pointing to them.

'That's the problem isn't it?' Cecil asked, 'There were quite a few people who would have readily done it given half a chance including myself!'

Irvine patted him on the hand to pacify him.

'The real question is who would have planned it out so precisely? That's what we have to look at. It was cold blooded and pre-meditated murder!'

They all sat back in their chairs and thought about the statement Irvine just made. He was right Susie thought. This wasn't a murder that happened in the heat of the moment. This was calculated and planned. She racked her mind to think who would have done it. Who would have been so precise?

Her mind kept returning to the Americans, so she had to ask.

'I am not sure if I mentioned it last time,' she started. 'But do you know anything about gambling debts that Mr Foley may have had?'

Cecil and Irvine looked at each other across the table. The look didn't go unnoticed by Susie. It was like they were reading each other's minds. She raised her eyebrows at them suggesting they should spill the beans.

'Well I'm sure he had debts everywhere!' Cecil said and turned his back on Irvine. Susie sensed he was fuming about the money they had loaned to Foley. Money they were unlikely to get back.

Susie remained silent. A technique she learned in a corporate training many years ago. Ask a question and remain silent. People can't help themselves but to fill in the blanks. Mostly she had used the technique to get the best gossip.

Irvine shuffled uncomfortably in his seat. Then finally broke.

'He did have a bit of a problem with gambling, yes.' Irvine said.

Susie remained silent.

'A bit of a problem?' Cecile scoffed.

'Well alright Mr Sulky, it was more than a bit of a problem.'

He went on to explain that Foley had developed a serious gambling problem in the United States. He said it started with the one arm bandits and progressed to poker. He had started frequenting the Late Night LA Casino. The problem was it was being run by some bad types. It started out as a manageable problem. It soon became compulsive gambling. The owners of the casino allowed him to clock up three hundred thousand dollars in debt before they stopped his line of credit. Shortly after that they called the loan in.

'Which he had no hope of paying off!' Cecil added.

'If he sold the house he could have, lovey.'

Cecil sighed. Selling the house was what he told them he would do a year before when they loaned him money. But no For Sale board had appeared on the property yet.

'Do you know much about these people he owed the money to?' Susie asked. She had taken out a notebook and written down the name of the casino. It sounded like a backyard operation to her but she decided she would have Meg research it on the Google.

'Not really, only that they were connected with some criminal gangs.'

'I see,' Susie said still writing.

'He came to see us a few weeks before the opening night of Castaways!' Cecil added. He had turned around to face them but the look on his face suggested he was still sulking.

'Yes that's right,' Irvine continued, 'he did look worried then about it all. Big mess he had gotten himself into, really.'

'Did he mention anything about these Americans he owed money to?' Susie asked.

'Not really, only as much as we have told you,' Irvine said.

'Well that gives me something to go on at least.'

Susie explained to them that the reason she had come to ask was the email threats and menacing phone calls to Mandy. She didn't let on that there were good reasons to suspect the Americans were here in the area to collect the money. The last thing she wanted to do was start a panic.

'Poor love,' Irvine said empathetically.

'Oh please,' Cecil rolled his eyes and sighed at the same time.

Susie raised her eyebrows once more.

'She probably had every reason to do it to,' Irvine tried to make light of it.

'Well she didn't want her father to sell the house to pay off his gambling debts. That was her home!' Cecil said rather firmly.

'Surely she wouldn't want to kill him over the matter though?' Susie asked. She highly doubted it, but thought it was better to check as the girl was staying with her. Last thing she wanted was a murderer in her keep.

'Oh she had far greater motives than that!' Cecil stated.

'Really?'

Irvine shot Cecil a look that suggested he was in trouble the minute Susie left.

'We swore to James we would never tell, sorry.' Irvine said.

Susie wondered what on earth it could be? She decided not to press the matter with them any further for the moment.

'Well I must be going, thank you for the tea.' She said standing up. They both stood up together and thanked her for dropping by. Irvine said it was lovely to have company as they didn't get many visitors.

'May I have a look at your conservatory briefly?' she asked. She said she was thinking of adding one to the side of the castle in a place that would have a delightful view across the lawn down to the rotunda.

'Of course,' said Irvine and led her through the lounge and out to the conservatory.

Cecil followed them and picked up a rag and a small container of oil. He had one of the rifles out on a table and had dismantled it. He was busy cleaning it as Susie and Irvine talked about the conservatory.

'Well I must go, are you off hunting then?' she asked.

'Oh, the annual fox hunt next weekend. Up at Lord Hammersmith's in Devon.' Cecil explained. 'These haven't been cleaned in an age so I am getting them all ready.'

'Yes it should be fun. His Lordship knows how to put on a shoot.' Irvine added.

Susie smiled and walked past the gun case in haste. As she did, she took stock of the rifles in the cabinet. Of the five there were three still in the cabinet, and one that Cecil was working on.

She thought nothing of it and bid them farewell.

18

After leaving Irvine & Cecil, Susie decided she didn't want to go straight home. Instead, she drove back through the town of Marazion and took A394 to the east. A few miles out of town she came to the small township of Roseudgeon. There she took a right-hand turn down Trevean Lane, past Trevean Farm to the end of the road.

She had read about Acton Castle in one of the books Mildred had returned. Given that she was living in Ash Castle, she thought it would be quite fun to find other castles in the area and meet with the owners. Perhaps form a little group of castle owners. A few days ago she had managed to pluck up the courage to call a Mr Trengrouse who is the current owner of the castle.

John Stackhouse, a marine biologist, had built Acton castle in 1773. The name came from his wife Susanna's surname, Acton. After Stackhouse's death the castle was owned by Vice-Admiral Praed who was Lord Nelson's navigator during the Battle of the Nile in 1798.

Mr Trengrouse was pleasant enough on the phone Susie had thought and said he would welcome a visit and a chat. Eager to make new friends in the area Susie had suggested she would drop in after her visit to Marazion.

Susie pulled her Land Rover up to the gates of the old castle. Her windows were down and a strong ocean breeze coming from Mount Bay filled her nostrils with salty air. She breathed it in and felt good to be alive.

Acton Castle stood proudly on the hill overlooking the bay. She imagined it would have a splendid view of St Michaels Mount, and further to the east to Lizard which jutted out on the Cornish peninsula. The castle itself had one central tower made of Cornish granite, and two wings added later also made of Cornish granite. It had beautiful manicured gardens with water features and fountains. The southerly side of the castle had gorgeous rolling hills down to the cliffs that fell away to the ocean below.

Nearby was Prussia Cove which had a history with smugglers being active in the area for many years.

Mr Trengrouse was standing by the front door waiting on her arrival. Susie concluded he must have seen her car coming down Trevean Lane. She thought there probably wasn't a lot of traffic that came down the lane most of the year.

He waved to her as she parked the car, undid her seatbelt and stepped outside.

'Greetings Lady Carter!' he called out to her as she walked across the paved parking area to the steps. She took the steps and shook his outstretched hand, returning his greeting.

'So kind of you to see me at such short notice,' she replied.

'Oh, it's my pleasure. We don't get many visitors these days,' Trengrouse said. He led her inside and proceeded to give her the grand tour. They made their way through the hallways, stopping to visit each room. Each room had its own story, and he proudly shared the story with her.

Mr Trengrouse was 83 years of age. His body was lean and a little on the frail side Susie thought. At times he was unsteady on his feet. His mind though was sharp as a tack. He had a great memory, and she sensed he was well educated. His wispy grey hair was long at the back and in the fringe which hung in his eyes. He kept blowing at it to remove it from his eyes but it always returned. He was wearing navy blue slacks, a black shirt, and a grey woolen cardigan. Probably his favourite cardigan Susie thought.

'The old castle is steeped in history then,' Susie said at one point.

'Oh, aye, a lot of history best not spoken of as well!' he laughed. The tour continued through to the kitchen which we had modernised about a decade ago he informed her. At the time his wife Sybil was alive. It was her last wish before she passed that they do something about that horrible old kitchen. Sadly she passed away before he had it finished. Now every time he goes in there he feels closer to her.

They sat down outside by the water feature to enjoy a cup of tea and some homemade Hevva cake. He had made it himself he told her rather proudly.

Susie loved the view across the bay and the fact that the castle was perched on top of cliffs that went down to the ocean.

'Is there a path down to the ocean there?' she asked.

'No, not here sorry,' he replied. 'It's a little too dangerous here. The cliffs just drop away and are quite dangerous. There is a cove below though.'

'Oh that sounds interesting?'

'Yes it's only a small one, and you can't see it from land so well.'

Susie was fascinated as she had started reading one of the books returned by Mildred on Smugglers in this part of Cornwall.

'Is that one of the Coves that the Carter brothers used then?' she asked.

'Well the story goes they did, and the other one over at Prussia Cove. That's why the older brother John was known as The King Of Prussia.'

He went on to explain that the Carter brothers would from time to time use Acton Castle as their hideaway when the law was chasing them. Stackhouse was often away travelling the world so the castle would be empty for months at a time. He would let the brothers use it in his absence.

Susie was all ears. As a young girl she had loved to read the Enid Blyton books such as the Fabulous Five which would often feature stories of smugglers tunnels.

The Carter brothers, Trengrouse informed her, were notorious smugglers and used Prussia Cove, mostly. Legend tells of the tunnel from the cove up into one of the small farm houses on the hill. He explained they worked for several years making the tunnel and it turned out to be a great source of profit for them for many years.

Susie asked if there were any smugglers tunnels from the cove below into Acton Castle, given that the Carters had spent considerable time there.

'Rumour has it yes. Some older folks around town claim that stories of smugglers tunnels into the castle had been passed down from their great grandparents.'

'Ooh that is exciting!' Susie said.

'Yes, but I have never found an entrance here in the castle to such.'

'Perhaps it had been boarded up over the years?'

'More than likely. There is a cave down below that could have been an entrance to a tunnel for sure.'

They chatted some more about the history of the area and all things to do with smugglers.

Susie asked if he was aware of any smugglers tunnels in the village of Polmerton.

'I've always been under the impression that the Smugglers Inn had a tunnel running down to the harbour there, but I've not checked it out myself.'

He explained to her that there was a local historical society in Polmerton. Councilor Bradshaw had been president, until the unpleasant business with the Mayor. Perhaps they might know more information as they were always looking into such things he informed her.

'Let me get you their details,' he said and shuffled off down a hall. A moment later her returned with a slip of paper. On it was written the name Janet Brown. She was listed as the Secretary of the society.

'Oh thanks, I know Janet from the Castaways play,' Susie said and paused a moment as the memories of the night came flashing back.

'Quite a messy business all of that,' Trengrouse said.

'Indeed, yes!'

19

'We have asked around town and there have certainly been plenty of sightings of them,' the Inspector informed Susie.

She had made her way back from Acton Castle, via Prussia Cove, to the police station in Polmerton. She had intended to drop in and see Hunter to discuss the details of the next cooking class to be run. Unfortunately, he wasn't in at the time, so she decided not to let the trip go to waste. She walked the three doors from the bakery to the station.

The Inspector said he had Constable Daniels visit every retail store in town to ask if anyone had seen the American tourists. They had managed to get a reasonably detailed description of them from Mandy, and Patty had added a few more details. So with a detailed profile of the two American men in question, Constable Daniels set out on foot. He walked into each shop in turn and asked if they had dealt with the Americans.

'Anything positive for us to go on then?' she asked.

'Nothing solid I'm afraid, other than the fact that they have been seen around town,' the Inspector replied. 'Seems they have been busy playing the tourist and all!'

Susie asked if they had any way of tracking them down, or information on where they might be staying. Unfortunately they hadn't been able to find out much. The last sighting of them was more than a day ago so it was possible they may have even left town the Inspector informed her.

They talked briefly about not having much else to go on in the case. Susie suggested that they should go back over and interview all the witnesses again. Perhaps see if they missed anything in their original statements.

The Inspector thought it was a good idea however they didn't have the resources to do so. With the annual Pirates & Wenches Convention happening in town at the moment they were stretched to the limit. He told her the convention brings in hundreds of extra tourists for the week but the police department didn't allocate any extra resources to them to help out.

Susie felt his frustration as he sighed. She sensed he would love to get a breakthrough in the case but had nothing really to go on, nor the man power to follow it through.

'I can see you are busy Inspector,' Susie said sensing it was time to leave. 'Now don't you worry, leave it to me!'

'Now wait just a minute Lady Carter. We have chatted about you getting involved in police business before, haven't we now?'

'Yes you are quite right,' she smiled at him. She bid him farewell with a promise not to meddle in police business.

The way she figured it though, if they weren't investigating the matter currently due to a lack of man power, then she wasn't really meddling in anyone's business.

She smiled to herself at the logic of it as she headed back out to the street.

As she walked along the street towards the car parking area, she thought to herself that she really wasn't sure which way to go with finding the killer. The most logical at this point was the Americans who had threatened Mandy. But if they couldn't be tracked down, then there wasn't much to go on.

She decided that a call to Margery might be in order. It seemed that whenever she felt stuck with such things Margery was always there to help her get a fresh perspective. The decision was made. She was going to call Margery as soon as she got home.

As she arrived at the car park on the edge of the village, she noticed a man that looked like Karl Lightfoot sitting on the park bench overlooking the harbour. She was sure it was him except he somehow looked older and more frail. He was hunched forward pulling his jacket tight around himself to protect him from the ocean breeze. A cigarette drooped from the corner of his mouth. Unshaven and looking like he hadn't showered in days Susie was reluctant to go up to him to say hi. She couldn't be sure what his frame of mind was.

She thought it would be best if she did though. The poor man had gone through enough in the last week.

'Mr Lightfoot, are you okay?' she called out from her car.

No reply came. Perhaps he didn't hear her she thought. She walked a little closer and tried again. This time he caught her voice over the wind.

'Lady Carter, and how are you today?'

'I'm fine Mr Lightfoot but I am worried about you?' she said. She took a seat on the bench next to him.

They chatted for a bit and he explained he was having trouble sleeping at night. So he came down here by the harbour to escape. The shooting of James Foley was haunting him at night. As much as he disliked him the last thing he would want was to harm him.

Susie listened patiently as he talked. She knew from experience that sometimes all people need is someone to lend them an ear.

He talked it all out and got it off his chest. She noticed he heaved a sigh of relief now that he had got it off his chest.

'Mr Lightfoot, do you have any idea on who might have wanted to do it then?' she asked.

'I've been giving it a lot of thought,' he replied but didn't continue. She waited while he gathered his thoughts.

'It could have been any one of a number of people,' he said. Susie nodded in agreement.

'But as I heard that the bullet was the type that came from a rifle there is only one person who came to mind.'

'Who's that then?' Susie asked. She suspected she already knew the answer.

'Well it's obvious then, isn't it?' he asked. 'It had to have been somebody who had a strong reason to hate Foley, and the knowledge of rifles. It would have taken a pretty good shot to hit him with such accuracy. And keep in mind the shooter was back stage, so he had to fire the shot over my shoulder and between me and were Patty Malone stood. Plus he had to hit a moving target. So it must have been someone who knew a bit about shooting.'

She waited not responding, leaving him space to say the name.

'It had to have been Cecil Miller!'

20

On the short drive from town back to the castle all Susie could think about was the accusation from Lightfoot. She questioned his state of mind as he looked like he hadn't slept in days. No doubt the stress of being falsely accused for the murder had taken its toll.

But Cecil? Could he really be the one?

Mr Lightfoot had no solid evidence to go on. He explained to Susie that it was more of a hunch than anything. When she pressed him further to explain he had told her that Cecil was wildly jealous of Foley. In fact, he was jealous of the affection that Irvine showed towards him.

Was that enough to justify murder then? She asked herself.

It was true that Cecil said he would have done it himself given half a chance. He had made the rather bold claim at both her visits. She had discarded the statement as just talk. She couldn't imagine in her wildest dreams that either Cecil or Irvine would be the type of people to commit cold-blooded murder. They didn't have it in them.

Then of course there was the matter of money. Money can make normal people do strange things Margery would always say. It was a saying that she had taken from her mother. Her mother often cited the quote after one of their neighbours when Margery was at the age of five, stabbed her husband to death for taking a shilling from the house keeping money.

'Indeed, money can make normal people do strange things!' Susie said out loud to herself as she rounded a sweeping bend. It was her favourite part of the journey as she could see all the way across the ocean to Lizard jutting out into the water.

The matter of the money loaned to Foley was clearly a factor but was it enough to drive Cecil to murder? And to do it in such a risky manner in front of all of those eye witnesses.

She decided that for the moment she wouldn't pursue the matter any further. There was simply not enough evidence to start pointing the finger of blame at poor Cecil. If the matter developed and further evidence against him came to light, then well and good, but until then she decided that Mr Lightfoot might well be wrong with his accusation.

Finally she made it home and parked the Land Rover in the garage around the side of the castle. She came in through the laundry entrance and took her coat and boots of.

Max had heard the Land Rover coming up the drive and was beside himself with excitement. He came running into the laundry, grabbed one of her boots and shook it all around like it was play time. He ran down the hall to find Meg and show her what he had, then came bounding back to return it.

He received plenty of attention from Susie who hugged him and scratched the back of his head.

'Max I do believe you have been putting on weight!' Susie said. Then she checked herself in the bathroom mirror and decided that she too was putting on weight. Too many tea parties she told Max.

'Perhaps we both need to go on a diet?' she asked him.

He cocked his head to one side as if confused by what she had said.

'Yes I guess you are right, I was planning on curling up with a good book, a cup of tea and a scone or two this afternoon. What about you old boy?'

Max barked in delight. It sounded like his second favourite thing to do. His first was clearly walking in the woods behind the castle. This sounded like a good plan to him though.

After saying hello to Meg and Mandy, who were looking at wedding magazines, she asked Woolsworth to bring her afternoon tea to the lounge. She went upstairs and slipped into something more comfortable for lounging around the house.

It wasn't long before she was curled up in front of the open fire. Woolsworth had placed the tea on the coffee table in front of her and stoked the fire. It crackled and spat a couple of times before settling down.

Max waited until Woolsworth had left. With the coast clear he jumped up on the couch and curled up at her feet.

Susie picked up the book 'A Smugglers Guide To Cornwall'. She was excited to read all about the history of smuggling in the area. Her chat with Mr Trengrouse at Acton Castle had her mind racing with possibilities. She read with great interest the many escapades of the smugglers from hundreds of years ago.

Polmerton was mentioned in the book more than Susie thought it might have been. It seems the town was once a haven of illicit activities. It made sense, she thought to herself. The surrounding area was littered with old abandoned tin mines. She imagined the miners would have come into town on their days off and the first place they would have headed would have been the local inn.

At the inn, over an ale or two, no doubt they would have made the acquaintances of one or two friendly locals eager to sell their wares to them. Avoiding paying the exorbitant taxes of the time would have appealed to anyone.

She read on to discover that many of the smugglers tunnels were thought to have been dug by tin miners themselves. In modern times engineers had studied the construction of the tunnels and marvelled at what a good job they had done. So it was naturally concluded that only those in the mining trade at the time could have pulled off such a great engineering achievement.

No doubt the tin miners who helped create the tunnels were well rewarded for their efforts.

She was annoyed with herself that when Constable Daniels was down in the cellar at the Smugglers Inn that she didn't get him to look further into the old tunnel entrance he had found.

He had suggested it looked like no one had been in there for years, but she felt he was perhaps a bit too reluctant to venture in for a closer look.

She made up her mind that she was going to go for a closer look herself.

First though she would research as much as possible so she knew what to expect.

Susie called out to Meg. She could hear her and Mandy in the kitchen chatting about their dream weddings, and where they would go on their honeymoons. She smiled to herself when Meg said she would want to go to Paris. Ever the romantic she thought. Mandy had said without hesitation that she would most like to go to Australia. She had seen a documentary on TV about a place called Noosa where wealthy Australians, and celebrities from overseas, would visit for their holidays.

Meg came to see Susie.

'Sounds like you two are having a jolly good time?' Susie asked her with a smile.

'Oh we are. Just like sisters really,' Meg smiled back. Susie was pleased. Meg was as happy as she had seen her since she arrived at Ash Castle.

Susie asked Meg if she could get on the Google and do some research. Find out anything she could about smugglers tunnels in Polmerton, and also anything to do with smuggling at the Smugglers Inn.

Meg agreed to do it right away. She loved doing research. In recent times she found she also had a fondness for helping Susie solve crimes though she hoped there wouldn't be any more after this one.

Before long Meg and Mandy were working as a team at the keyboard.

Susie called out to Woolsworth that she was going to need a top up on her tea, and perhaps an additional scone or two.

She went back to reading and half an hour went by.

It wasn't long before Meg returned to the lounge room with Mandy following. They had done a considerable amount of research and printed off some useful information.

'Here this will interest you,' Meg said and handed Susie a print out of a newspaper article. The article was dated from six years ago.

Tunnel To Harbour Discovered the headline of the article claimed.

The article from the Cornish Times told the story of how a small cave in the rock face to the north end of the harbour had proven to be the entrance to a tunnel. Sand drift over the years had largely blocked the entrance. A recent king tide however had caused the ocean to surge and wash away a lot of the sand. It left exposed an entrance to what many had long believed to be a smugglers tunnel.

The local historical society was called in to further investigate. They managed to send one brave young soul by the name of Billy Bradshaw, grandson of Councilor Bradshaw who was the President of the society at the time, into the cave and enter the tunnel itself. Sure enough he made his way through to what looked to be a cellar. Later it was shown to be the cellar of the Smugglers Inn.

Billy had reported the tunnel to be in remarkably good condition despite smelling rather putrid. Billy was hailed as a hero for his efforts.

A large photo of Billy with members of the historical society showed them at the entrance to the cave. Susie recognised Councilor Bradshaw and Janet Brown in the photo but not the other members. Meg filled in some others names for her.

'If you want more information, perhaps contact the historical society,' suggested Meg. She handed a print out to her from their website with the contact details. Janet Brown was now listed as the President.

'I might just pay Janet a visit then and see what else she can tell us,' Susie said. 'Then we might organise a little search party of our own!'

Meg's face lit up with delight. She loved the adventure of it all.

21

Hunter arrived at three thirty that afternoon for a planning session with Susie. They were getting behind on their plans for the next cooking school class and felt they best get together and decide on the agenda, amongst other things.

The timing however suggested that afternoon tea would be on offer. As usual, he brought with him some delightful treats from the bakery. He was certainly one to spoil her, Susie thought. She tried to resist, but the temptations were too strong.

Meg and Mandy joined them for a cup of tea in the dining room.

Woolsworth appeared with a tray loaded with cups, saucers and a large pot of tea. He had been busy dusting and had not taken off his floral apron, much to the delight of the girls.

'Nice you have been able to stay here a bit Mandy,' Hunter said making small talk. He had no idea why she was staying over but could see that Meg and Mandy were getting along grand. They were both of a similar age and looked like sisters together.

'Oh I have a bit of an announcement to make,' Hunter said as he polished of his tea.

'Do tell?' Susie asked.

'Well, I was contacted by a charity group that take in women from domestic abuse homes, terrible business really,' Hunter said.

He went on to explain that they wanted to raise awareness and much needed funds. They had contacted him to see if the 'Famous

Polmerton Bakery' could help in any way. After thinking about it and chatting it over with them, he came up with the idea of the worlds largest tea party.

'You know, like a Guineys Book of Records kind of thing,' he continued. 'We host the worlds largest tea party. It would raise money for the ladies, and would no doubt get lots of press coverage for our little venture as well.'

'What a wonderful idea!' Meg said with joy. She loved a good party, and everyone loves tea.

'It does sound exciting,' Susie agreed, 'but where would you host such an event?'

Hunter smiled a big wide smile and winked at her.

It took Susie a moment to realise what he was thinking. Then she cottoned on.

'What? Here?' she asked just a little shock.

'Here is about the only place we could hold it,' he informed her, 'besides it would be for the ladies and all.'

Susie laughed, 'And how many are we talking Mr McGill?'

'Well I've been doing a bit of research. In order to break the record we would need about one hundred people over for afternoon tea!' Hunter said as he loaded another scone with fresh local jam.

'Oh my, one hundred people here?' Susie asked a little shocked.

'Well that's what I was thinking. You could open the castle up for the day and charge them all to take a tour as well. Raise some more money.'

'Let me give it some thought!' Susie said.

After tea was finished Susie informed the girls that she and Mr McGill had business to attend to. Emma had invited them to Newquay for dinner, and to talk about her wedding dress, so they both went off to get ready.

They watched them head of like two excited school girls.

'Good to have you all to myself now,' Hunter smiled at Susie when quiet had returned to the castle. He reached out and put his hand on hers.

'Oh I do worry about them,' Susie said as she watched Meg drive off down the driveway and out through the gates.

In her younger years she never really felt maternal. The opportunity didn't present itself as she hadn't met the right man to marry. So besides having dogs to love, like Max, and a few friends she never really had to worry over the safety of someone she cared about. Watching Meg and Mandy drive off into the afternoon though she now knew what it must feel like to have a child you cared so deeply about.

'Cheer up now, they will be back soon!' Hunter said breaking her train of thought.

'Right, yes,' she said.

'Nice girl that Mandy Reed. You would never know she was the daughter of that man!' Hunter said firmly.

'Yes, it does sound like he was a bit or a wretch. Owed a few people money as well.' Susie said.

'Oh he owed everyone money, he did. Owed the bakery two hundred pounds for his lunches!' Hunter laughed, 'I guess we will never see that money now.'

Susie was shocked to hear it. She wondered if she shouldn't start keeping a tally of everyone he owed money to. She thought about telling him about the money owed to the Americans, and the threats made to Mandy, but then thought it best not. The fewer people who knew about it the fewer people who might be in danger.

'It's a shame about what happened,' Hunter said his thoughts drifting off.

'About the murder you mean?'

'Well yes that, but no I mean to her.'

'To Meg? Or to Mandy?'

'Mandy.'

'What happened to her then?' Susie asked.

'Oh you don't know?'

'I'm not sure really, what are you referring to?'

Hunter went on to explain that about ten years ago when Mandy was about fourteen she was in the family home alone. Foley had come home drunk. He had been in a right state over the last couple of days. Only a few days had passed since he arrived back from Hollywood on another unsuccessful trip trying to land some acting work.

Apparently Mandy had been sitting in the lounge, not expecting him back until much later. She was painting her toe nails and was only wearing her bra and panties. Foley was so drunk he forgot for a moment where he was. Hunter explained he forced himself on to her.

'Good heavens, do you mean?'

'Yes he raped her, apparently!'

She had managed to fight him off as he was so drunk and went running to the neighbours two doors down. The neighbour at the time was Sally Dewhurst. Hunter explained that Ms Dewhurst was working for him in the bakery at the time which is the only reason he knew about it.

'Did she involve the police? Press charges at the time?'

'No. She told Ms Dewhurst she couldn't go to the police.'

'Oh dear,' Susie sighed

'Wouldn't surprise me if it wasn't the only time!'

Susie was shocked by the news. It was as Hunter had said, ten years ago, but such wounds can bury themselves deep in your mind and affect a person.

'I don't know how the police are going to solve his murder then,' Hunter said. 'It seems like everyone had a reason to do it!'

Susie nodded her head slowly.

'Yes even his own daughter!'

22

Janet Brown lived in Helston which was a short fifteen minute drive from Polmerton. Helston was an old market town to the northern end of the Lizard peninsula. The town itself was home to more than eleven thousand people making it a decent size. It was a good place to base her business Janet had said when she moved there more than six years ago.

She had spent most of her life living in London working in the West End theatre district. She had some notoriety as the best dressmaker in London and was always in demand. For more than twenty years she had made costumes for some of the biggest live theatre productions to come to the UK including Cats, Wizard of Oz and more. She loved the theatre but in the end the hectic pace of it all wore her out.

Six years ago she decided to go for a quieter life. Everyone told her how wonderful her dresses were and over the years she had developed many loyal and repeat customers. With her track record she had confidence to start a fresh new life in Cornwall.

Helston had been where she was originally born and brought up for the first three years of her life. Her mother was a seamstress and when her father died young in a fishing boat accident, they moved up to London to find work.

It seemed the logical place to return to. She packed up her possessions and made the move six years ago and she felt it was the best decision she had ever made. Being rather frugal she had saved up some money and managed to purchase a neat little brown stone cottage in Church Street. From her new home she could easily walk into town to get her messages.

Susie had called ahead that morning to see if it would be okay for her to pop by. Janet readily agreed. She informed Susie on the phone that she didn't get many social visits. Any time she had visitors it was usually for a fitting for a new dress. So she was delighted to have her visit.

Helston was a busy little village Susie decided as she navigated her way through town. She found Church Street and made a left-hand turn into it. A few minutes later and she passed Janet's place. It was easily identified by the 'Browns Dress Maker' sign hanging in the window. The road was narrow and winding with few parking spaces. She ended up finding a parking spot about ten houses down the street.

Finally she arrived and Janet greeted her with a big hug in the door way. She led Susie inside and closed the front door behind her.

The front room of the house was where she did all of her work. It was loaded with large rolls of material of all manner of colours. Against the wall was her workbench with a sewing machine, and in one corner was a mannequin used to pin up new creations.

'The light is very good in this room you see,' Janet informed her as she gave her the tour of her working area.

Hanging up were two rather extravagant looking capes made from a deep red velvet. Susie commented on them and discovered they were being made for Irvine and Cecil. Matching capes for a fancy dress party they were to attend in Brighton in a few months.

'Oh sounds like fun,' Susie said admiring the stitching in them.

'They certainly know how to have fun!' Janet replied.

'Have you known them long?'

'Oh yes, for years. Worked with them on and off in the West End.'

She led Susie down the hall to the reception area out the back. A modest kitchen and a small dining area opened up to a medium sized lounge. It felt smaller than it was as one wall was lined with bookshelves. Books were piled high in every nook and cranny of the bookshelves.

'Looks like you have some interesting books here?' Susie said as Janet filled the kettle.

'Oh I do love to read yes, mostly history books really.'

Susie searched through the books and found quite a few books on the history of the Cornwall area. She found the one penned by her late Uncle Charles Ash III titled 'The History Of Polmerton'.

On the inside cover she found a hand written dedication to Janet from her uncle.

'Personally signed. It was from the book launch at the old book store in Polmerton. Gosh that would have been shortly after I moved here.' Janet said as she set the table.

'I must read it soon,' Susie said.

'Oh take that one to read,' Janet offered.

Susie told her she had a copy at the castle returned recently by the Aunties. They had a good laugh at the Aunties who knew everything about everyone including everything that went on in Polmerton.

They took a seat as Janet poured the tea.

'And how have you been getting on dear?' Susie asked. 'You were rightly very upset on the night of the opening.'

Janet took a moment and poured milk into her tea. She nodded as Susie asked the question. Susie imagined she had probably been expecting to be asked.

'Oh yes, I was very upset. It was such an awful thing to have happen,' Janet replied.

'Oh yes a great shock to us all!'

'Well I wasn't shocked that he was murdered in the end. Perhaps just in the way it happened!'

Susie asked why she wasn't shocked he was murdered. Janet explained that there was probably a good many people around who had issues with James Foley. And no doubt one of them had taken the opportunity.

'I was surprised though they let Mr Lightfoot go!' she said.

'Oh, you think he was the guilty party?'

'Well I mean, it looked that way didn't it?' Janet said and sipped on her tea. She thought about it for a moment longer before adding, 'And they hated each other. Karl was always jealous of James you know!'

'Yes I see what you mean, the problem was forensics said the bullet didn't come from the prop gun Karl had in his hand though,' Susie explained.

'You mean there was a second shooter?'

'Well one shooter, but it wasn't Karl Lightfoot that is for sure.'

'I don't see how that would be possible though,' Janet said thinking out loud, 'that would mean someone would have to bring in another gun, and smuggle it out again at the end!'

Susie explained that was partly the reason for her visit. She told Janet she wanted to pick her brain as to her knowledge of the area. She reached into her handbag and produced the print out that Meg had given her. The photo showed the local historical society members gathered at the entrance to the cave near the harbour in Polmerton.

'Oh yes I remember that exciting time like it was yesterday. Wait one minute.'

Janet got up and walked down the hallway and into one of the rooms. Susie could hear her moving boxes around and sighing before she returned with a small cardboard box. On the side in thick black marker she had written 'Historical Society Stuff'.

She plonked it on the table and opened the lid.

Susie stood up and looked at the treasure trove of things she had stored in there. Old photos, maps, and newspaper clippings. She found a small photo album and flicked through it showing Susie different photos of the meetings of the society.

She handed the photo album to Susie who continued to flick through it while Janet dug deeper into the box. Toward the back of the photo album she came across a photo of James Foley standing in front of the Smugglers Inn with his arm around Janet. They looked extremely well acquainted Susie thought.

'Oh my!' Susie exclaimed as she found even more photos of the two of them together. It was like seeing the woman standing in front of her posing with a ghost.

Janet looked up to see what Susie had gasped at.

'Oh that, yes. We were quite close at one time you know,' Janet said dismissively.

'Oh I didn't realise.'

'Yes at one point he took an interest in local history and the like. But it didn't last long. Not much with James ever did.'

Susie closed the photo album and placed it to one side.

'Here it is!' Janet said happily. 'This is what I wanted to show you.'

She moved the box and the cups of tea to one side. In the vacant space she spread out the hand drawn map in front of Susie. It was a map that showed the entrance to the cave which led to the tunnel. It showed how the tunnel made its way up the small incline of the hill, and then snaked its way practically under the police station, under the road and into the cellar of the Smugglers Inn.

'It's rumoured that at one stage one of the Carter brothers was in the lock up in the Polmerton police station. The other two brothers used the tunnel to start a branch of it right into the cell and broke him out.' Janet laughed.

Judging by the laugh Susie wasn't sure if the rumour had any truth to it, but she made a mental note to check in with the Inspector.

She studied the map carefully and traced her fingers along the path of the tunnel from the Smugglers Inn to the cave on the north side of the harbour.

'Is it hard to find the cave entrance?' Susie asked.

'Oh yes it is, it's mostly blocked in these days with sand and rubbish. People don't even notice it as a cave, more like a hole in the rocks if they notice it at all.'

Susie nodded. Her mind was ticking over considering the possibilities.

'I can see where you are going with all this then,' Janet said.

'You can? I am not sure myself,' Susie laughed.

'Oh yes, you are thinking that is how the murderer escaped!'

'What? Through the tunnel?' Susie asked alarmed.

'Yes! Makes sense doesn't it?'

Susie thought about it for a moment before responding.

'Yes, I guess it does!'

23

Susie bid farewell to Janet an hour later. They had a good chat about everything that Janet knew about the history of the area. She certainly was a wealth of information Susie had told her.

They agreed to speak with Patty Malone, and if she was willing, they would organise to have the tunnel searched from both ends. Susie explained that Constable Daniels had looked in the cellar but did not venture into the tunnel itself. They both felt that Patty would be more than willing to oblige. The last thing she wanted was an unsolved murder at the Smugglers Inn on her hands.

'It would just add to all the others!' laughed Janet.

Involving the Inspector and the police was discussed as part of the search. Susie felt they might get further if they didn't involve them at this stage. She explained to Janet they were rather busy with the influx of tourists for the Pirates & Wenches Convention in town.

Besides which, she really wanted them to focus on finding the two Americans who were threatening Mandy. The last thing she wanted was to distract them from that mission.

Susie stepped out onto the narrow street. A chilly wind was blowing up the street and caught her by surprise. Her skin reacted to the ice cold air. She pulled her jacket closer and wondered why she didn't bring a scarf with her. She looked across the horizon in the direction of the ocean and saw storm clouds brewing.

'I must get home before that storm takes to land,' she muttered to herself. She quickened her pace towards her car.

'What's that dear?' a familiar face called to her from the front door of her house. Susie had parked her Land Rover in the parking spot outside her door.

She looked up startled not realising anyone was within hearing distance.

'Oh just talking to myself I am afraid,' Susie laughed and fumbled for her car keys in her bag. 'Old age I'm afraid!'

'Not as old as some Lady Carter,' the lady in the doorway replied. They both laughed at the idea.

'I'm sorry, have we met before?' Susie asked not wanting to be rude. She knew the ladies face was familiar but she couldn't place her.

Mrs Pettlebottom introduced herself to Susie. She explained that they had met at the opening night for the Castaways musical. They had been introduced by Mable & Mildred Milford who she was well acquainted with.

'Oh yes, of course, how are you dear?' Susie enquired.

Susie feared the worse. She remembered that Mrs Pettlebottom was a talker. On the opening night of the play she felt stuck in a corner with her as she went through every year of the Castaways play sharing stories and more. She feared Mrs Pettlebottom might be quite the gossip as well.

At 82 Mrs Pettlebottom was frail to look at. She had several wispy grey hairs protruding from her chin, and three missing teeth. Her back was slightly stooped causing her to walk with a shuffle. Some of her neighbours would joke that you could hear Mrs Pettlebottom coming by the sounds of her shuffling feet.

'Not too bad dear!' she replied, 'I see you have been visiting with the dress maker then?'

'What? Oh yes Mrs Brown.' Susie agreed. 'Checking to see if she is okay after the incident the other night.'

'Oh it was a business wasn't it? Poor Mr Foley!' she sighed.

'Terrible business I'm afraid!'

'I was rather fond of him you know!'

'Oh you don't say? How well did you know him?'

Mrs Pettlebottom explained that she would often see him here. In fact he would park in that very spot that Susie's Land Rover now occupied. She had asked him once what he was up to in a town like Helston.

He responded by saying he liked to get all of his clothes tailor made. As a Hollywood star he had a certain appearance he needed to keep up. Word around the acting community was that the dress maker in Helston was the finest there was. So he would come for fittings, and to discuss the latest styles with Ms Brown.

'You don't say?' Susie responded. She was all ears.

'Oh yes he loved a nice suit jacket that was hand made you know!'

'How often would he come by?'

'Oh I don't know, let me think now.'

She tapped her bony finger to her chin as she thought back. After a brief moment she decided that at one stage he was coming by several times a week. That was a year or two ago. Then she didn't see him for at least a year.

'All of a sudden a few weeks ago he came for another visit!'

'Maybe the break was due to him being in America for a bit?' Susie asked.

'Possibly yes. He was an actor you know?'

'When he came by a few weeks ago, did he seem okay?'

Mrs Pettlebottom thought about it some more. After a few moments she agreed that yes he seemed his normal self when he arrived. He had taken some time to chat with her which was always nice she explained.

She went on to say that he had told her he had come about his costume for the Castaways play. Something about needing a new fitting.

Susie glanced at her watch and then to the brewing storm in the sky. She decided she best make haste which meant she was going to have to cut Mrs Pettlebottom short.

'Well, lovely to chat, but I really must be on my way before this storm hits!'

She had her car keys in hand and was opening the door as she said it.

'Yes of course Lady Carter, lovely to chat. Drop in again some time soon!'

'I will do. Good day Mrs Pettlebottom,' Susie said with one leg in the car. She was about to swing her backside into the drivers seat.

'The last time he was here of course they had an awful commotion.'

Susie stopped and stood back out of the car.

'Why was that?'

'I'm not sure entirely. I just heard them yelling at each other for a bit.'

'Did you hear why?'

'Not really. He told me as he passed he wasn't happy with the stitching on his vest.'

James Foley did have an awful reputation as being a hot head and a perfectionist. She had seen some of that side of him come out during rehearsals. He had even grumbled at her for standing in the wrong spot at one stage.

So she could imagine if he wasn't happy with his costume then he wouldn't hold back from letting all and sundry know about it.

He was after all in his twilight years and he didn't have many opportunities left to ignite his acting career. Every detail would have mattered to him Susie thought.

'Well a good day Mrs Pettlebottom!'

Susie got in the Land Rover swiftly and closed the door before she could be dragged back into any more conversation. It was nice to make a new acquaintance around town, but one must be mindful of time she reminded herself.

She peered through the windscreen at the dark clouds above the town of Helston.

Rain started to fall as she sped away.

24

Susie made it back to Ash Castle in good time. She parked her Land Rover and could hear Max barking with excitement at her return.

She made her way inside via the laundry entrance so she could slip out of her jacket and boots. The dash from the garage into the laundry was just long enough to ensure she was thoroughly drenched from the driving rain.

Outside thunder clapped overhead. It cause the ground the castle was built on to shudder. The hairs on the back of Susie's neck stood up as a cold chill ran down her spine. It had gone dark outside as the storm clouds rolled in. Wind howled in the eaves of the castle extension. Lightning lit up the sky in random spasmodic episodes.

Susie was glad to be back in time despite her soggy condition. She took a fresh towel out of the linen press and dried her hair.

Max's muffled barks could be heard somewhere but she couldn't make out where exactly they were from.

Upstairs she changed into dryer more comfortable clothes. She intended to have a night curled up in front of the fireplace. Reading with a nice cup of tea and an open fire were one of those simple pleasures in life she cherished.

In the kitchen she asked Woolsworth to prepare her a snack and a pot of tea. The smell of burning oak wood from the fire place in the lounge had pleased her. Woolsworth certainly had a good sense of timing as he always seemed to know when to light the fire before she had a chance to ask.

'Ma'am I think you should check in with the young ladies. Seems they have had a bit of a fright!' Woolsworth informed her.

She found them already in front of the fireplace. Mandy had a look on her face like she had seen a ghost. Meg was busy comforting her. They were cuddled up together on the couch and Susie was sure that Mandy must have been crying.

'Hello you two, how is everything?' Susie asked taking a set opposite them.

Max plonked himself down on the rug in front of the fire. His fur glowed from the heat of the fireplace.

'We have had a bit of a fright!' Meg explained.

'Oh dear, what is it?'

Meg explained that as they were coming up the road to Ash Castle, they passed a rental car coming out of the castle. There was no where else they could have come from. Mandy had said they were the same two men who she had seen waiting for her in her driveway.

'To make matters worse, one of them pointed at me as they drove by!' Mandy blurted out before sobbing.

Susie looked at Mandy and thought the poor girl was frightened out of her mind.

'Are you sure it was them?' Susie asked.

'Quite sure!'

'Right!'

Susie leapt to her feet. She marched over to the small desk in the corner of the lounge and took the phone off the hook. The local police station was already programmed into the phone on speed dial. She pressed #7, and the phone dialled right away.

A moment later she returned to the lounge chair.

'Constable Daniels will be right over to check the area,' Susie stated. She didn't think she would have any problems getting Daniels to come as he was ready at a moments notice to visit the castle.

Woolsworth arrived with tea and some snacks. He placed the tray down on the coffee table.

Susie explained they might need something a little stronger to which Woolsworth readily agreed. He headed to the cabinet where the tawny port was kept and came back with the bottle and three glasses.

He poured each of the girls a glass.

Susie found a notepad and pen.

'Now then girls, describe them to me in as much detail as you can?'

They were able to give remarkable descriptions. Mandy was able to recall a great deal of the facial features of the two men, especially the one who had pointed at her in a threatening manner.

Susie wrote it all down.

Ten minutes later Woolsworth showed Constable Daniels into the lounge room. Susie thought he looked rather dapper in his police uniform.

'Hello then!' he said to the ladies.

Meg leapt up, ran to him and gave him a big hug. Susie smiled to herself as she watched his face go bright red.

'Oh my, you're soaking wet!' Meg said and led him to the fire place.

'Now what seems to be the bother?' he asked. He had his pocket notebook and pen at the ready to take down any details.

For the next five minutes Meg and Mandy took it in turn to describe what had happened. They were convinced the two Americans had been at the castle snooping around and no doubt looking for Mandy.

He wrote it all down, nodding in encouragement. He was a great listener and had endless patience. Unlike the Inspector who had none and was busy counting down the clock until his retirement. Susie thought Constable Daniels would soon be doing a fine job as Inspector Daniels of Polmerton.

Susie handed him the detailed descriptions of the two Americans that she had written down. He read it over before folding the paper to place in his pocket.

'Right oh then, I best go check the perimeter of the building. Make sure it's all secure and there is no sign of these two American suspects then!'

They watched as Woolsworth led him around the castle checking windows were locked. Then he headed outside with the aid of a bright pink umbrella that Woolsworth had lent him. Through the window they could see him doing a complete search of the outside of the castle. Despite the umbrella he still managed to get about as wet as he would have without it.

Fifteen minutes passed before he knocked on the front door.

They all rushed to see him.

He had folded the umbrella up and placed it dripping leaning against the wall. He himself stood there dripping wet.

'How did you go?' Meg asked him, 'Oh you poor thing you are proper wet you are!'

'Right, I've checked everything, and all looks secure.'

Right then his radio burst into life. First it crackled and splattered with white noise. That was followed by the sound of a grumpy Inspector calling for the Constable's help. The Inspector was having some trouble with some unruly Americans causing trouble at the Salty Pirate Inn. The Salty Pirate Inn being the only other pub in Polmerton.

'Oh my!' Mandy exclaimed.

'That could be them!' Meg shrieked.

'We don't know that for certain now, there are a lot of tourists in town. Ever since that Pirates of the Caribbean film came out, everyone thinks they are a pirate!' Constable Daniels sighed.

'Be careful!' Meg said.

'Right oh best be off then,' the Constable said.

They all watched him rush across the courtyard to his police car and drive off into the pouring rain.

25

Susie suggested that the best way to take their minds of things was to play Monopoly. It had been her favourite board game growing up. Meg and Mandy readily agreed so they set up the dining table with the game. Susie also brought the bottle of tawny port and glasses. It seemed a good night for it she told them.

As they started the game Susie told them all about her visit to see Janet Brown. She explained the map and how the historical society had found the long lost smugglers tunnel some years ago. Meg asked if they could go in the tunnel but Susie had to inform her that the cave entrance at the harbour may not be readily accessible. She suggested that they should get together a party though of the three of them, Max and Constable Daniels when he was off duty. Together they might just be able to get access.

'Sounds like an adventure,' Mandy said as she purchased Park Avenue.

'It does sound rather grand,' Meg agreed.

Susie told them that she had a hunch that whoever the murderer was could have used the smugglers tunnel to discard the rifle used. It would of course require them to have knowledge of the tunnel in the first place.

'But I think it's quite common knowledge that at some point there was a tunnel to the Inn,' Meg added. 'I mean most folk around here would be aware of that!'

'True enough,' Susie agreed. She wondered why then Patty Malone was less forthcoming with information on the tunnel and its existence.

Mandy explained that Patty was reluctant to confirm its existence because when the story came out in the local newspaper she was inundated with people wanting to come take a look. They came from far and wide. Some even came down from Glasgow, and some from France. Once man even arrived from Florence eager to explore the tunnel.

'Oh why so much interest then?' Susie asked.

'Apparently back in the 1780's the Carter brothers had taken possession of a trunk full of gold. The story goes that a ship was sinking of the cost near St Michaels Mount. They went to the rescue, but the crew had abandoned the ship already. In the storm they all swam to the safety of the harbour. But the Carter brothers boarded the ship and found the trunk of gold.'

Mandy went on to tell the story of the ship having returned from The Caribbean. They had stolen the trunk from some locals down there. The story passed down through the years was that the Carter brothers couldn't use their usual hiding places as they were under constant pressure from the local police at the time. So they came around to Polmerton and hid the trunk in the tunnel.

Not long after one of them died from pneumonia, one was arrested and thrown in jail, and the other disappeared never to be heard of again.

'So the treasure is still burried in the tunnel then?' Meg asked in disbelief.

'So the story goes!'

Susie sat back in her chair. Now she understood why Patty was reluctant to let her explore the tunnel. The last thing she wanted was treasure hunters arriving at all times of the day or night.

It was her turn to role the dice. She moved the hat piece four places and landed on a run of Meg's hotels. The rent for the stay was more than Susie had left in the bank. As she was out of the game, she told them she would go and make hot chocolate for them all.

Susie walked out of the lounge and down the hall towards the kitchen. Max followed along with his tail between his legs. His least favourite thing in the world Susie would often say, is thunder storms.

Outside the wind howled around the castle and out buildings. It was pitch black outside and the belting rain showed no signs of letting up. Thunder continued to rumble and explode in the sky. The dark of the night was interspersed with brilliant light as it danced across the night sky.

'It's all right Max,' she said stopping in the hall. He came up to her and stood close by. His soft fur was still warm from laying to close to the open fire as Susie gave him a reassuring pat.

They continued on their way when she thought she heard the sound of someone knocking on the front door. It sounded more like desperate banging between the thunder claps she thought, but who wouldn't be desperate to get in out of the rain.

'That must be the Constable returning,' she said to Max.

A detour in their journey took them to the grand hallway. She could see two figures silhouetted in the night sky through the frosted glass.

'Oh he must have the Inspector with him!' she said out loud.

She walked towards the front door, hand outstretched reaching for the large brass door knob. All of a sudden the loudest clap of thunder she had ever heard in her life shook the whole castle. The chandelier light fitting above the stairs shook so hard Susie thought it might break free from its fitting. Terrified she reached instead for the stair handrail and held on until the shaking stopped. Max had retreated to a corner under the stairs behind the knights armour.

Once it passed she walked back to the front door. She reached out again for the brass knob and just as she turned it, her hand feeling the cold of the door knob, all the power went out.

Caught off guard Susie swung the large front door open wide.

'Hello Insp...' was all she managed.

There standing in the door way was not the Inspector and Constable. Instead it was two strangers. Without the aid of the light, and only the bolts of lightning to assist, she could barely make out their faces.

What she could make out though terrified her no end.

The two men standing before her seemed to be a perfect fit for the two men Mandy had seen in her driveway. She was sure this was the two Americans!

Terrified she took three steps backwards from the door.

She went to scream but nothing came out. All she could manage was to put her hand to her face as if to stop a scream escaping.

On seeing Susie step back the two Americans stepped forward.

'Evening Ma'am!' the shorter older of the two spoke. He had a Yorkshire style cap on and he made the gesture of tipping it towards her.

They were dripping wet. Both wore long grey trench coats reminiscent of Dick Tracy. Their boots were muddied.

In shock Susie had unknowingly taken two more steps backwards. It left more than enough room for them both to step inside and close the door behind them.

'Sorry to frighten you Ma'am, you look like you have seen a ghost,' the American continued. 'Our car broke down. About a mile down your road. We saw your light on and wondered if we might use your phone?'

Susie had to think fast. She decided she couldn't push them back out the front door. They were too big and strong for her to do that. Instead she would need to use her wit to led them to think she was the only one in the house. In the interim she could get Meg and Mandy to go out the back door and take her car to go and find the Inspector.

'Oh dear, yes you both looked drenched to the bone,' she said.

Off the entrance hall to the right was a reception room that they hardly used. Susie had felt it was too formal to take visitors into it to meet with them. She much preferred the comfort of the lounge room and dining on a rainy day, or the rotunda in the garden if the weather was looking promising.

The reception room sat unused most of the time. Now was a good time to make an acception she had thought to herself.

'Yes the storm isn't showing any signs of letting up!' the American replied.

'Come this way,' Susie said and led them into the reception room.

They followed her to the right and a short walk down a hallway that was rarely used. She found the door and opened it up. Her nostrils were greeted with a musty damp smell. Woolsworth had taken the liberty of covering over all the antique furniture with white sheets to keep them from gathering dust.

'Have a seat here gentleman,'

As instructed, they both sat down.

'We really don't want to bother you Ma'am, just if we could use your phone to make a call,' he said fidgeting in his seat. He went on to explain that they had been out all day taking photos on their cell phones and run their batteries flat.

The hire car they were driving veered off the road. The rain had gotten so bad that they couldn't see a corner coming up. Instead of taking it they splashed into a puddle deeper than they thought damaging the front left tire. It caused the car to pull hard to the left and slammed them into an embankment. They needed a tow truck and a lift back to town.

'Oh with this power out I'm afraid the phones here will not be working,' Susie replied. Her mind was thinking over time. She had to delay them while at the same time not allowing them to know that Mandy was in a room down the other hallway. 'Let me see if I can find my mobile phone, I hardly ever use it!'

'That would be great thanks,' the American nodded.

'Oh, and I will make us a warm drink. You two look like you could use it.' Susie added as she walked out. The reception room was freezing cold, and she noticed they were shivering from it in their wet clothes.

Outside In the hallway with the door closed she whispered to Max. She told him to stand guard at the door and to bark loudly if they tried to leave. He wagged his tail. She was sure he understood.

Susie rushed back into the entrance hall and took the other hallway. Trying to be as quiet as she could she turned the corner at the end and found the lounge.

'The Americans!' she said in a half scream of terror.

'What? Where?' Meg asked jumping to attention. Mandy also leapt up and panic filled her face.

'I have them in the reception room!'

Susie explained that as she went to make the hot chocolate, she heard the knock at the door. The two silhouetted figures at the door led her to believe it was the Inspector and Constable returned.

'What are we going to do?' Meg asked.

'Right, Meg you head to the kitchen and grab the keys to my Land Rover. Then come and get Mandy here and head out the laundry door. The Land Rover is parked in the small garage outside. You will be protected from view. Head into town and find the Inspector and tell him I have the two Americans here in the reception room.'

Meg took off before Susie had finished explaining the plan. She bolted to the kitchen. As she was only in her socks, she could run on the old wooden floor boards without making a sound. Seconds later she was back and grabbed Mandy by the hand. They took off together to follow Susie's instructions.

When she saw the lights of the Land Rover backing out Susie headed to the kitchen to put the kettle on.

A few moments later she returned with a mug of hot tea for them both. The older American was standing. He was trying to take in the antique paintings but in the broken light it proved difficult to make out the details.

'Big fans of castles!' he stated as he took the mug from Susie.

'Oh, you don't say?' she responded.

'Oh yes! We came all the way from LA to check out some old castles around here. Perhaps if you don't mind we could take a look around?'

Susie felt sick at the idea despite the fact she knew the girls had gotten away safely.

'Well we occasionally open up for visitor days,' she replied politely, 'but mostly it's a private residence!'

The American nodded and exchanged looks with the other one. The second American appeared to be growing impatient. They both sipped at their teas which Susie had made piping hot. So hot that their lips burnt on the rim of the metal camping mugs she had found.

Susie sat on a seat by the door and watched them. Max sat in front of the door. An awkward silence followed. In her mind she tried to calculate how long she would need to delay them. The girls were going to need to head into town, find the police in one of the establishments, get their attention, and then bring them back here. Could be at least twenty to thirty minutes she felt.

'How did you go with that phone?' the older American asked. He had placed his tea down as it was too hot to hold on to. Now he was starting to pace back and forward. Max watched him moving back and forward, with his tongue hanging out to one side.

'Oh, sorry! No good I'm afraid. Without power the main phone won't work. And I can't seem to find my cell phone anywhere.' She gave an uncomfortable smile. 'So what brings you to our little neck of the woods then?'

The older American went and sat back down.

He told Susie how they were lovers of all things Castles. When they heard about the Pirates & Wenches Convention happening in Cornwall, they jumped at the chance to be involved. They had spent the entire day driving around looking at all the castles in the Cornwall area, and old historic homes.

Susie nodded and listened to his story. It sounded somewhat convincing she thought, but she knew better!

'Girls!' the younger of the two American's blurted out. It startled Susie as he hadn't spoken until this point.

The older American turned to the younger one and patted his hand on his knee, 'Yes Jeffrey, we did see some girls didn't we!'

26

For the next twenty minutes Susie managed to engage them in small talk. Despite her fear growing by the minute, and her heart beating in her chest, she managed to at least give the appearance of remaining calm.

She told them all about the castle, and the area around Polmerton. At least as much as she knew of it. They seemed rather interested in her tales of the smugglers at Acton Castle. She asked if they had been yet to which they replied they hadn't but it was on their list. The story of the Carter brothers delighted them, or so it appeared.

The thought did cross her mind that they were surprisingly good actors. Clearly they had no interest in the castle and history of the area at all, yet they engaged in conversation for some time before they both appeared to become agitated and impatient. The only sign that they may be up to no good was the younger one of the two blurting out the word 'Girls' to which Susie had promptly ignored.

'Damn this storm!' the older one said getting to his feet again. He continued his pacing. 'I really need to get to a phone, are you sure your cell phone isn't working?'

Susie stood up as well. Over his shoulder behind their backs she could see headlights snaking their way up the road that led to the castle. It was a mile long and had a number of twists and turns that slowed most drivers down. In a storm it was extra difficult to navigate.

'Oh I am sure the power will be back on shortly,' she reassured them.

The younger one was starting to fidget in his seat. There was a large puddle on the floor under his feet that was mixing with the mud from his boots.

'We saw two ladies driving here earlier in the day,' he finally stated not able to hold himself back any longer. 'Are they staying here at all?'

Susie faked a look of surprise at the idea.

'Oh no, just me and Max here I'm afraid.'

Max sat up to attention at the sound of his name. He wasn't sure what was going on but this get together seemed out of the ordinary.

The two Americans exchanged a look across the room. The older one appeared annoyed at the question. The younger one stood up unable to sit still any longer.

'Are you sure about that?' the younger one asked.

Susie noticed out of the corner of her eyes that his hand was in his right-hand side pocket of his jacket. There was a large object in the pocket that he clearly had taken in hand. He had taken a step towards her starting to look more menacing.

She gasped. Her heart rate accelerated and the sound of the beating drum rang in her ears. Fear raised another notch. She had no idea how to answer the question.

'Oh yes, quite sure!' she said from her seated position.

'Just that I wanted to meet the one in the passenger seat. The one with the long auburn hair. She looked nice!' the younger American said and grinned wide. His large frame filled the center of the room.

'I'm not sure who you mean sorry dear,' Susie replied. Max could sense her fear and he came and sat at her feet. Not his usual lounging pose slumped across her feet. He was fully alert and on guard. He sat between the menacing stranger and Susie.

'Yes I think you know exactly who!' he said and took another step closer.

Max growled a low guttural warning kind of growl. Susie noticed the hairs stand up on the back of his neck. He was getting close to launching. She placed her hand gently on the back of his collar to reassure him.

Her palms had become sweaty. She prayed inside that the police would come soon. The younger of the two Americans had reached a point beyond being polite. He was now becoming threatening. She feared for her safety.

'I am sorry young man, but I am certain I have no idea what you are talking about!'

'I want the girl,' he replied talking over her. He didn't register what she had said, or just plain didn't believe her. It was clear now why they were there.

He shuffled forward another step.

'Jeffrey,' the older American said with a tone that suggested he take it down a notch.

Susie could hardly breathe. Her muscles in her arms and legs had seized with tension.

With that the door to the reception room burst open. It startled all of them.

Susie jumped to her feet in fright.

'All right, what is going on here then?' the Inspectors voice boomed in the room. His large bulking frame filled the door way. He marched into the room with Constable Daniels following. They moved Susie out of the way and confronted the two Americans.

Meg took Susie by the arm and they scurried away to the safety of the lounge room. Susie had never been so relieved to see a friendly face in all of her life. She hugged Meg in front of the fire place and tears welled up in her eyes. Max pushed his head against her leg to comfort her. For a brief moment Susie sobbed letting out the stress and emotion. It wasn't long before she regained her composure.

'It's all right now love,' Meg said in a reassuring voice. She held Susie and gave her a gentle pat on the back.

'Where is Mandy?' Susie asked.

'I dropped her off to Hunter's. I saw his light on. She was terrified poor love, so I called in there and he was more than happy to look after her for a bit.'

'Oh good heavens!' Susie said.

With that the power was restored. The lights came on in the castle chasing the darkness away.

Having regained her composure Susie headed back out towards the grand entry hall. She was just in time to see the Inspector and the Constable leading the two Americans out the front door in handcuffs.

'I want that girl!' the younger American said as he was marched off by Constable Daniels.

27

Susie slept barely a wink that night. She & Meg had sat up with Max in the lounge room late into the night playing Rumey. They had both been shaken up by the events of the evening and felt it best to wait until they were really tired before trying to go to sleep.

Eventually the storm died down outside which they both felt a lot better about.

Finally at about one am Susie got into bed. Max had been snoring at the end of her bed for the last thirty minutes while she got ready.

When she did finally go to bed, it was a broken night sleep. She tossed and turned and the voice of the younger American taunted her,

'I want that girl,"

The next morning she awoke later than usual. Meg was already in the kitchen eating scrambled eggs made by Woolsworth. A large mug of black coffee sat in front of her with steam wafting from it.

Susie greeted them both and sat down opposite Meg. Before she had a chance to settle into the seat Woolsworth presented her with her breakfast. Hard boiled eggs with runny yolks, and toast cut into fingers. This was accompanied by a pot of tea.

She quickly drank two cups of tea before tackling the eggs and toast.

'First things first,' she said to Meg, 'we need to go and see if young Mandy is okay!'

Meg looked up from her paper she was reading. She nodded in agreement.

'Poor girl must have got a heck of a fright,' Susie continued.

'I just spoke with her on the phone,' Meg answered, then went back to reading.

Susie sat there waiting for the rest of the statement but there was none forthcoming.

'And?' she eventually asked.

'Oh she's okay, seems like she had a good nights sleep,' Meg said.

Susie sensed she was upset or frustrated.

'Everything okay dear?'

Meg ignored her at first. She had that look that suggested she was in a huff about something. Susie had learned though not to push her when she was like this. Eventually she would open up and share what was on her mind.

A moment later Meg looked up from the paper and sighed. She put the paper down and picked up her mug of coffee.

'I don't know,' Meg sighed some more. 'It's like he doesn't even notice me.'

'Who doesn't dear?'

'Constable Daniels of course!'

Meg explained that when she went to get the police last night he was all formal like. He called her Ma'am and didn't show any affection to her whatsoever. The least he could have done was give her a hug to help her calm down.

'And then last night when they arrested the two Americans,' she continued, 'he didn't even come back to say good night to me at all. To see if I was okay. He just hopped in the car and off he went!'

Susie listened and nodded in agreement at all the right spots.

'It's like I don't even exist!'

She was getting herself worked up and emotional. For no good reason Susie thought. Susie was confident that the Constable was more than keen on Meg, but he was equally awkward about how to approach her or show his feelings towards her.

'Well he was very busy last night,' Susie suggested. 'And he was on official police business. It's a serious matter you know.'

'I suppose so,' Meg sighed again, 'but I just wish he would give me some sort of indication of how he feels about me!'

Tears started to well up in her eyes and she ran off to the bathroom.

Susie didn't want to interfere in the natural course of events or young love, but she wondered if she shouldn't give the young Constable a bit of a hurry along.

An hour later Susie and Meg were in the Land Rover heading down the hill towards town. The last of the tourists from the Pirates & Wenches Convention were heading out of town as things had come to an end the day before. Susie was looking forward to things returning to normal in town and being able to find a parking spot.

The whole trip into town Meg talked about how strong her feelings were for Constable Daniels, and how frustrated she was that he was so slow in expressing his.

Susie explained that sometimes young men need a bit of time to come around.

They managed to get a park outside the Famous Polmerton Bakery. Hunter was behind the counter and greeted them both with a cheery hello and a beaming smile.

'Things are looking up around here then!' he proclaimed. 'My two favourite ladies in the world, right here in my humble establishment!'

Susie laughed. He could be a character and a charmer when he wanted to be.

They asked after Mandy and Hunter explained she was okay. She had slept well and was in good spirits this morning. She had the lunch shift at the Smugglers Inn and had left ten minutes ago.

Meg decided to pop across the road and see that Mandy was okay.

'Oh you have had a night then?' Hunter asked.

'Indeed. Gave me a bit of a fright!'

Susie updated Hunter on all that had happened in between him serving customers. She went into detail about the storm and the power going out. She told him how the castle shook with each clap of thunder as the rain pelted down. As she told how there was a knock at the door and she had thought it was the Constable, she got herself all worked up again. Finally she got to the part about the police returning and taking them into custody.

'Oh my, what a fright you must have had!'

'Yes it was rather, and they put up a protest at being marched off in handcuffs I can assure you.'

'I imagine so, yes!'

Susie watched as Hunter counted out ten Heeva Cakes for a customer, and three of his famous Cornish Pasties. Trade was steady given the tourists had all started leaving town which was good news.

'Now do you think they had anything to do with the incident though?' Hunter asked returning his attention to her.

Susie explained what Mandy had told her. There was a sizeable debt involved with gambling back in Hollywood. She didn't doubt it was reason enough for murder. If he had refused to pay up, or to sell the house to pay up, then yes she could see there was sufficient reason for foul play.

'Ahh yes, indeed. Shame really,' Hunter sighed.

'What's that?'

'What's what?'

'The shame?'

'Oh right, yes well, shame the police let them go this morning.'

Susie must have had a look of fright on her face. She felt the blood drain out of her head and into her legs.

'They let them go?'

'I think so yes, I saw them walk by about an hour ago! I didn't dare tell Mandy who was out the back at the time.'

Horrified at the thought Susie marched out of the bakery.

28

Susie marched the two shops up the street and burst in through the front door of the police station. She was fuming mad that they had let the Americans go and she was determined to find out why.

As her eyes adjusted to the dim lighting in the police station, she found the Inspector with half a mouthful of scones fresh from the bakery. It was ladened high with jam and cream. He paused halfway through taking another bite startled by the sudden commotion.

Constable Daniels was sitting at his desk in the corner processing paper work. Recognising there was trouble brewing he put his head down and burred himself in busy work.

'What is the meaning of this Inspector?' she demanded. She closed the door behind her with the heel of her foot and marched across the office floor. Standing over him she tried to convey the idea that she was not going to back down until she had answers. Answers that were satisfactory!

'Take a seat now Lady Carter,' the Inspector said and gestured with his hand toward the seat. For a moment she stood there fuming with hands on her hips. Then she realised a seat was probably not a bad idea after all. She sat down with a thud and a sigh.

'Well?'

'Scone?' he asked pushing the plate towards her, 'fresh this morning.' He grinned at her and finished the rest of the scone in his hand.

'No thank you!'

'Come on now, the bakery boy made them.'

Her mouth watered at the thought. Hunter did make great scones there was no doubting. But this was serious business. People's lives are at stake she reasoned in her mind. My life was in jepordy, not to mention young Mandy's. But they did look nice, and she was sure the cream was from one of the local diaries as well.

'Well maybe one,' she said and took a scone.

The Inspector leaned back in his leather swivel chair. It creaked under his sizeable frame. He folded his hands behind his head and asked her what the trouble was.

She explained that she had just now heard that the two Americans who had threatened Mandy's life had been released from custody. It was not right she said to him. How could the police be so incompetent as to let them go? Not only did they threaten Mandy, and scare the life out of her, they were also likely the best suspects for the murder of Mr Foley.

'Mistaken identity,' the voice of Constable Daniels interrupted her. He had stood up and gathered his keys and cell phone. He headed out the door in a hurry.

'Mistaken identity?' Susie asked the Inspector.

'Apparently so, yes!'

'But weren't these two the Americans that had been threatening Mandy?'

'Doesn't look like it no, they are American to be sure, but not the ones who might cause harm to young Mandy.'

The Inspector went on to explain to Susie the extensive interview process and detailed back ground checks both he and the Constable conducted over the course of the night. It turns out the two Americans were indeed castle enthusiasts. The older one, the father, was head of the American Castle Lovers Association, or ACLA as it is known. They had visited for the convention and were driving around town photographing old castles and historical homes in the area.

The younger one was the son, and he wasn't quite right as the Inspector put it.

'But, what about him saying he wanted the girl?' Susie asked a little confused.

'Mind of a five-year-old sadly.'

The Inspector continued saying that nothing in their background checks amounted to any wrong doing. If anything the father was a pillar of society back home in Los Angeles. It seems that they were wrongly accused. Fortunately they weren't to put out by it all and saw it as a great adventure to share when they got back home. And according to the stamp in their passports they hadn't arrived in the country until the day after the Castaways opening night.

'Right I see, well, this is a little embarrassing I am afraid!'

'No need to apologise Lady Carter. You did the right thing being on the side of caution and all,' the Inspector smiled.

Susie returned his smile rather awkwardly. He offered her another scone to which she readily agreed. As she bit into its creamy soft fluffy texture she determined once again she must start on a diet soon.

The Inspector joined her and finished off the last of the scones.

'Now Lady Carter, was there anything else?' the Inspector asked. She could see they were both rather busy. They had been all week with the convention on, and by the sounds of it neither of them had got a chance to sleep last night.

'Oh no that's all, sorry to disturb you,' she said apologetically.

'Not at all Lady Carter.' The Inspector said standing up. She always knew when the conversation was over with the Inspector.

He walked her to the door.

'Inspector there was one other thing,' she said unsure how to word it.

'Gone on then?'

'Well it's about the young Constable.'

'Oh? What's he done now then?'

'Actually it's what he hasn't done,' Susie said.

She explained of the brewing love interest between the Constable and her Meg. He agreed he had noticed the twinkle in the lads eye of late. She explained how upset Meg was that he didn't appear to be having the same feelings for her, or at least not expressing them. He nodded in agreement stating that it was important you knew where you stood in such matters.

'So I wondered Inspector,' Susie continued, 'given you are a man of the world.'

'Oh aye, when it comes to matters of the heart,' the Inspector objected.

'Yes in your day, you would have been quite …'

'A lady's man,' the Inspector finished her sentence. He puffed his chest out as he said it. 'Yes I was known to attract a few of the local ladies indeed!'

'Yes well, could you have a word with the Constable, maybe give him a nudge along?'

'I certainly will. Might give him a few pointers as well.'

'Pointers?' she asked unsure.

'Of how to deal with the young ladies and all,' he said proudly.

'Yes that would be grand. Perhaps suggest to him that he takes her on a date and tells her how he feels.' She smiled.

'Oh right, make it official like. So they are going steady and all?'

'Exactly,' she said pleased he was catching on to her train of thought.

'Consider it done Lady Carter!'

29

Pleased with her efforts, though still embarrassed with the mixup with the Americans, Susie headed across the road to the Smugglers Inn. She wanted to see that Mandy was okay. And she was going to check with Meg and see if she wanted to stay for lunch at the Smugglers Inn.

She whistled out loud as she crossed the road.

Ducking her head she pushed the old wooden door open and stepped out of the light into the more dimly lit pub. The crowds had thinned out now, and it was back to its regular pace of locals and the occasional tourist.

A cheer went up with some locals as she entered. Meg, Mandy and Patty who were gathered at one end of the bar joined in the cheer. Susie felt her face blush at being cheered simply for entering the Inn. She smiled at everyone as she joined them at the end of the bar.

'Hello Patty, Mandy how are you dear?'

'All good Lady Carter. Just pleased that all was okay,' Mady replied.

A few moments later Meg and Susie were seated at a table in a window which had some rays of light breaking through. They were examining the menu's trying to decide what to have for lunch. Too many choices slowed the process down.

Patty Malone wondered over and told them about the Chef's special for the day. It was roast lamb with rosemary, and thick chips on a bed of mashed peas. The carrots slow cooked in honey, and thick layers of gravy to complete the dish. Patty described it in such detail both Meg and Susie found themselves becoming hungry at the thought. They both agreed the Chef's special was what they would have.

With Patty taking their order to the kitchen Susie shared her conversation with the Inspector. Not every word of it mind, she felt it best to edit the conversation to make it more palatable for Meg's delicate ears.

'I had a word with the Inspector about your concerns,' she started.

'Oh yes, he must think I'm just being silly now.'

'Not at all! In fact he shared that he has some experience in such matters.'

'Never?'

'Indeed yes, fancies himself as a ladies man!' Susie said, and they both roared with laughter. 'Any way, he assured me that Constable Daniels does indeed feel strongly about you. He's just been very busy this last week or so.'

'Oh that's nice,' Meg said, her face lighting up. Her smile was as big as it could be.

'Yes, and I asked if the Inspector could use his many years of experience to nudge things along a bit.'

'You did not?' Meg asked shocked but enjoying the moment.

'I did too!' Susie said, and they both laughed.

'So I can expect a proposal soon?' Meg said, her mind drifting off to a fairy tale wedding, and a dream come true.

'Well one step at a time young Meg,' Susie said.

They toasted to new love with their glasses of Savignon Blanc recommended to them by Patty. She had said it was the perfect wine to go with a roast lamb. The wine imported from the Hunter Valley region of Australia and was highly sought after but hard to come by in Cornwall Patty informed them proudly.

'Here's too young love!' Susie said raising her glass.

Meg raised her's, and they clinked glasses. 'Young love!'

The locals gathered at the bar let out a cheer to the cheers.

But neither Susie nor Meg heard it.

All they heard was the sound of screaming coming from the back store room.

A blood curdling spine chilling scream. And the scream came from Mandy.

Susie was first to her feet knocking over her wineglass. She bolted towards the end of the bar where the storage room was located around the corner. She knew that the storage room had a door that opened up to the small carpark at the rear. It was frequently used by staff and all the deliveries arrived there.

The storage room itself was fairly large. It was right next door to the kitchen. On one side where rows of shelving for canned and packaged goods. The other had a walk in cool room. It was large enough for the freezer, more shelving and could take two people in there at a time.

Susie felt her heart pounding as she covered the dining room area in record time. Startled on lookers had heard the scream and wondered what on earth was going on?

Thinking she was making a fast pace she was surprised to see Meg over take her.

Meg arrived in the doorway to the storage room first, followed shortly after by Susie panting and gasping for breath.

The first thing they saw was a terrified Mandy huddled in the corner with a look of terror on her face. Tears streamed down her face and she was trembling in fright.

'What on earth?' Susie asked as they both rushed to her.

That's when they heard the door to the storage room get kicked closed. A sickening thud as the door slammed back into the door

PIRATES, WENCHES & MURDER

frame. Susie turned her head in time to see the large bolt being slid across fastening the door secure. No one was coming in through that door any time soon she thought.

The second thing she saw was a handgun pointed at her face.

She went to scream but nothing came out.

Instead she instinctively backed up and put her hands in the air. Meg did the same. Her eyes darted from the locked door, to the gun, and around the storage room they were now a captive in.

'What on earth is the meaning of this?' Susie asked indignant.

'Take a seat lady,' the voice behind the gun instructed her. She went to protest but the look in his eyes suggested now was not the time.

Holding the gun was a well dressed man in his late thirties. He was handsome and athletic looking, yet his face told the story of a life lived on the wrong side of the law. Jet black hair was combed over stylishly, but it was the piercing black eyes that really struck her.

He gestured with the gun for Susie and Meg to sit next to Mandy. They quickly followed instructions with their hands still held high in the air.

Standing behind the man with the gun was a second man equally well dressed. He was older by about ten years Susie thought. He looked impatient, a man on a mission. He casually pulled a pack of cigarettes out of his suit pant pockets and extracted a cigarette.

'What is going on here?' Susie asked trying not to sound terrified.

'I want my money!' the second man spoke. It was a gravelly voice. The type of voice you developed after years of working in noisy environments and having to shout above the nose to be heard.

'What money is that?' Susie asked. It was more of a delaying tactic. She knew they had come to collect on the gambling debt from James Foley.

Mandy had been right in that there were two Americans who had been threatening her. Shame about the Father and Son who had come to the castle asking for help. Turns out they were quite innocent. Now the real menace was in front of them. Susie had no idea how she was going to get herself out of this mess.

'She knows!' the younger one with the gun said pointing to Mandy.

'I don't have your money, leave me alone!' Mandy shouted at them.

The older American lit his cigarette and took a slow drag on the end. He blew the cloud of smoke above their heads toying with them. Susie, who hated cigarette smoke, waved it away in disgust.

'Listen here, your old man owes me a lot of money. Either you are going to pay up or else!'

'Or else what?' demanded Susie.

The younger one pointed the gun straight at her. She got the message and sat back.

'Look, I am going to make this real easy for you. You pay up the money your old man owed me. If you can't pay, then you will have to sign over the deeds to his house to settle his debts for him.'

Mandy had a look of horror on her face. She wasn't about to sign the house over to these two, she would rather die than do it. She also didn't have the money to pay them. There was simply no money left.

'How much money are we talking?' Susie asked. She had heard muffled voices and noise outside the door. She was certain that with the police station just across the road that help would be here soon. The most sensible thing to do would be to stay calm and delay these two for as long as possible.

'Three hundred grand!' the older American replied and ashed his cigarette on the floor. 'Pay up or we take the house!'

'Yes well, the house title is not in her name so that is not an option!' Susie responded.

'No problem, I prefer cash.'

'Mr Foley was bankrupt. There is no cash to be had either!'

'Well then we have a big problem don't we?' the older one said. He took a step closer to Susie and blew smoke in her face. She coughed and indicated her disgust waving furiously at the cloud of smoke surrounding her head.

'I tell you what, how about you let the girls go, and then we can come to some sort of arrangement on the outstanding money?' Susie asked. She thought it was worth a try to see if she could get the girls free.

The older American laughed. He shook his head as he casually put one foot on a shelf to lean on and drew another long suck on the cigarette. He took a moment and looked at the three ladies on the floor. Susie wondered if he was unsure what his next move was going to be.

'I tell you what instead,' came the reply, 'How about you shut up! The three of you are coming for a little trip with us.'

He stamped his cigarette out on the floor and squished it with his foot. The back door had been closed, so he walked over and cracked it open slightly to peer out. A sliver of daylight poured into the room.

'Okay everyone up!'

The three ladies stood up. Susie watched as he pushed the door open wide enough to look out and survey the car park. There were three cars parked in the bays along with their large Ford Forte sedan.

He walked out into the daylight to the waiting car. After double checking there was no one in the car park he gestured to the others to follow.

'Move!' the younger one said from behind them. He pushed the gun into Mandy's back who jumped pushing into Meg who bumped into Susie. Susie got the message and marched across the car park.

Within a few moments Susie, Meg and Mandy were all lined up in the back seat of the car. The younger one took the wheel while the older one leaned over the backseat with the gun menacing them.

'Look, I don't know what you hope to achieve really,' Susie said, 'but if you let the girls go, I am willing to negotiate with you to pay off the debts myself!'

'Very kind of you Ma'am but I won't be letting anyone go I am afraid.'

The younger American negotiated the small narrow streets out of the town of Polmerton. He found the turn off that led to the top of the hill were the house was. He took a narrow right-hand turn and came across a truck almost at a stand still.

This was the steepest part of the road at more than forty five degrees. It was a killer to walk up, but Mandy had always said that people complimented her on her toned legs, it was because of walking into town and back up this hill.

The truck belonged to old farmer Harrison. He had a sheep station on the flat plains about five miles out of Polmerton. He would often try to avoid the tourists on the seaside road, and besides it took a good five minutes longer that way, so instead he travelled over the hill to get back to the farm.

Today his truck was weighed down with large straw bales. They were piled high above the cabin and wider than the trucks width. The narrow lanes around Polmerton didn't really accommodate this mode of transport so well. Either side of the road were large tall hedges making it impossible to see around the truck or to either side.

The truck groaned to a standstill and Harrison put the hand brake on. It groaned under the weight of the cargo in the back. Thick black clouds of smoke exited the exhaust and blanketed the car they were in.

Susie thought this was perfect as it would delay them and hopefully give time for the authorities to arrive.

'What in God's name is going on!' the older American cried out.

'Oh it's Mr Harrison,' Mandy replied, 'Looks like his truck has broken down again. We might be here for a while!'

'What kind of hick town is this, anyway!'

'Well you are not in LA now!' Susie added.

'Back this thing up and let's take another route!' the older American demanded.

The younger one did as he was instructed. He looked in the rear view mirror and noticed a small white Fiat coming up the hill behind them. In it was a rather tall man who looked like he was in his sixties. The fiat was struggling to get up the hill itself but it was closing in on them.

'Looks like we are blocked in here,' the younger one said.

'God damn it!' the older one said and slammed his fist down on the dash.

He unbuckled his seat belt and went to open the door to the car but it would only half open. They were stuck on a bend in a lane that was so narrow you couldn't fully open the doors on the car when you were stationary.

With the door half open he attempted to squeeze out. He managed to get himself out onto the road but was wedged in by the door. With some effort he pushed the door closed and got free from the car to the front. Susie watched as he attempted to get up the side of the truck to speak with Mr Harrison.

He was determined she would give him that much, but she worried he would ruin his nice suit against the hedge. Squeezing with all his might between the truck and the hedge he disappeared.

From her position in the middle of the back seat Susie could see the rear view mirror. She had recognized Inspector Reynolds right away even without his police hat. His hair was a little thinner than she had imagined, and what was left of it was a bit disappointing. Never the less she was filled with relief to see him.

With the older one gone with the gun and probably wedged between the truck and hedge, the Inspector made his move.

Susie watched as he swiftly exited the Fiat, and ran the distance to the drivers side of the Americans car. The younger American was caught up looking out for his colleague that he didn't even notice the Inspectors arrival.

With the window down the Inspector balled up his oversized fist and slammed it into the side of the head of the driver. Caught completely unaware the impact of the blow to the side of the head caused him to black out instantly. He slumped over in his seat held back by the seat belt.

Satisfied he wasn't moving the Inspector put his finger to his mouth to indicate silence to the three terrified ladies in the back. They all nodded. He then headed to the back off the truck and took up a position behind the rear tail lights listening for any sounds.

A second later there was movement to the side. Susie could see the hedge being pushed aside as someone was coming through. She held her breath. Frantically she pointed and indicated to the Inspector that someone was coming. No doubt it was the older American with the gun. For a brief moment she was frightened for the Inspector. He was twenty years the senior on the older American, and he had no gun. Meg reached for Susie's hand and squeezed tight. The three of them slid down in their seats.

The movement in the hedges grew closer. Now the final part of the hedge leaning against the truck was pushed aside.

'Right oh, keep moving I said!'

Meg squealed with delight. She recognised that voice.

Out of the hedges emerged the older American with his hands on his head. His face was red from pushing through the hedges. He had a black eye and swollen cut lip. Most importantly Susie thought, he had his hands on his head.

Behind him came Constable Daniels. He looked like he had been in a street fight and emerged victorious. He had the Americans gun, and it was now wedged firmly into the back of the American pushing him forward.

As soon as they emerged into the light, the Inspector pounced.

He whipped out his handcuffs and cuffed his hands behind his back. With his giant hand he pushed down on the shoulder of the American indicating for him to sit. Awkwardly he squatted to the ground and slumped against the rear tire of the truck.

With that the Inspector returned to the car, dragged the younger one out, and cuffed him to just as he was regaining consciousness.

The three girls squealed with relief. They burst out of the car and ran to give both the Constable and the Inspector huge hugs of gratitude. The Inspector blushed, 'All in a day's work now ladies.'

Meg squeezed her arms around Constable Daniels and pecked him on the check.

'My hero!' she declared.

31

'He is so brave!' Meg declared as the three girls all piled into the kitchen back at Ash Castle.

Max was so excited to see the three of them he wagged himself left and right. He went from Susie to Meg, and Meg to Mandy getting pats. His excitement led him to even try to get a pat from a reluctant Woolsworth. Max took the hint and continued to lap up the love from his favourite girls.

Woolsworth put the kettle on for them and made himself scarce.

'He certainly was,' Mandy agreed, 'the way he must have tackled him with the gun and all!'

'Yes we were very lucky the Inspector and Constable were nearby,' Susie added, 'No telling what might have happened!'

Mandy got a cold chill down her spine at the thought.

It wasn't long before they were all settled in the lounge with mugs of hot chocolate. The fire place was crackling away throwing off much wanted warmth. As happy as they all were to be back they were all a bit shaken up.

Max knew something was up though he wasn't quite sure what it was. He stuck close by Susie's feet to make sure she was okay.

They chatted about what had happened at the tops of their voices. As a result of the noise they hadn't heard Hunter arrive and park his car. He was shown in by Woolsworth carrying a large tray of his latest creations.

He greeted them all with his usual cheery welcome. They were all happy to see him and excited to see what he had on his tray. It was covered with a tea towel.

'I've got a surprise for you my luv,' he said to Susie holding the tray in front of her.

'Good heavens, what on earth is it?'

'You can do the honours then,' he said to her indicating to pull the tea towel off.

She whipped it off and the three girls all gasped with delight. The tray was full of rectangle shaped sponge cakes, dripped in chocolate, and sprinkled with coconut. The middle of each was layered with jam made locally. They were fresh out of the oven this morning.

'Oh my,' Susie said, 'what on earth are they?'

'Lamingtons my dear!' he said proudly. Susie took one and placed it on her plate.

Hunter offered them to each of the girls who happily accepted.

'Lamingtons?' Mandy asked never having heard of them.

'Oh yes, Lamingtons. An Australian delight!' Hunter said.

Susie took a bite, and it melted in her mouth. She closed her eyes and savoured the moment. Hunter watched on waiting for her response.

'Well?' he asked impatiently.

'Love it!'

'Me too!' said Mandy.

'Oh my!,' Meg added.

'Yes I noticed you were reading a travel magazine the other day, and you seemed rather interested in Australia, so I thought I would whip you up a little something.'

'Wonderful,' Susie said, but she was too pre-occupied to engage in conversation.

'Oh, and I bumped into Constable Daniels as I left town. He said everyone was to wait here and he would be up shortly to take your statements.'

They chatted for half an hour with everyone sharing their version of the story. Hunter listened with great interest to each account. He thought they were all extremely lucky to have gotten away unharmed.

Everyone agreed the Inspector and Constable were local hero's and should receive some sort of medal for rescuing them.

They were interrupted when Woolsworth showed Patty into the lounge. A round of cheers went up for her. Mandy rushed over and gave her a big hug.

'Oh, I just heard what had happened,' Patty said, 'I wanted to come and see if you are all alright, or not?'

For the next five minutes they recounted the story of being locked in the storage room, then being bundled into the car at gun point. Fortunately for the old farmer Harrison being broken down on the steepest part of the hill they all agreed.

'Oh so glad all is okay!' Patty said. She suggested they might put on a special evening dinner celebration to thank the hero's of the day. Everyone agreed it would be a splendid idea, and they started busily making plans for it. Susie suggested the Inspector might not welcome the spotlight on him, but too bad for him.

Patty headed off to go back to work. She told Mandy to have a day or two off to gather herself after her awful fright. Mandy said she was fine and would come in the next day.

Another half hour went by. They laughed and joked and had a good time. Hunter told them stories of all the weary tourists wondering in and out of the Famous Polmerton Bakery over the last week of the convention. Most of them had never eaten real food he told them so they were either stunned or delighted by his offerings.

Woolsworth appeared at the door to the lounge again.

'Ma'am, the Constable is here to speak with everyone!'

'Well show him in please Woolsworth!'

Hunter took the opportunity to take his leave. He explained he had plenty of work to do down at the bakery, and he didn't want to leave Aimee there on her own for too long. He bid them all a good day and took the empty tray from the much appreciated lamingtons with him.

Constable Daniels appeared in the doorway.

'Constable Daniels!' Meg squealed and rushed over to greet him. She wrapped her arms around him and squeezed causing him to blush. His face went bright red with embarrassment as she clung to him.

'Now now, I'm here on official police business,' he informed her.

Meg nodded and released her grip from around his waist. She gave him a quick peck on the cheek before returning to her seat on the lounge.

'Come and have a seat Constable Daniels,' Susie said and made room for him on the lounge. He sat next to Susie with Max at their feet, opposite the lounge where Meg and Mandy sat. Max placed one paw over the foot of the Constable which caused the girls to laugh.

Constable Daniels was all business. He told them they had detained the two Americans and were likely to charge them with possession of a firearm, threatening harm with a firearm, taking hostages, and resisting arrest.

'What about making threats and attempting to blackmail Mandy here?' Susie asked. She was determined to make sure they did their job thoroughly and that the two Americans were locked away for a long time.

'Right, yes, well that's why we need to get a detailed statement from all now,' the Constable said in agreement. 'I need every detail so we can fully understand what has taken place.'

He pulled out his notebook and a pen. Susie noticed it was a larger notebook than he had used previously. He was here to get all the details down which she was pleased about. She watched him as he went about the business of getting a statement from Mandy.

Susie was pleased at how thorough he went about the process. He had come a long way from the opening night when the Mayor was unfortunately murdered. At the time he was a little green and unsure of himself. Right now though he seemed to be a lot more confident, and he knew precisely what questions to ask and when. And he left plenty of opportunity for Mandy to speak and gather her thoughts at the right time.

An hour and a half later he had a detailed account of what had taken place.

'Right oh then, that should be enough to lock these two away for a long time!' he declared. He informed them that when it got to court, they would need to be present and called as witnesses which they all agreed to.

'Do you think they were responsible for the murder of Mr Foley?' Meg asked.

'Well it seems most likely, but we have to see what evidence there is against them.' Constable Daniels replied. 'It does seem like there was a strong motive for it with the debt and all.'

'Yes three hundred thousand would be enough to motivate many people to commit such a crime,' Susie agreed.

'Yes, plenty have done it for much less,' Constable Daniels said. 'The thing is we would need evidence they were in the building at the time.'

'Unless you can get a confession?' Meg asked.

'Oh aye, if they are happy to confess to the murder then that would do it for sure.'

Susie nodded in agreement. She hoped that it was them and that they did confess as it would wrap up the whole saga. They could all close the book on the matter and move on with their lives. Especially Mandy who was going to need lots of good friends to see her through the next few months, Susie thought to herself.

'Well I best be off then,' he said.

'Oh no, do you have to go so soon?' Meg asked.

Susie looked at Mandy and caught her eye. She suggested to Mandy that they should check on what Woolsworth had planned to cook for dinner. Mandy caught her line of thought and the two of them departed swiftly to give Meg and the Constable a moment.

32

Susie was sitting in the office sorting through paperwork. She had not realised just how much paperwork there would be when she started the Cornwall Cooking School with Hunter. She felt extremely fortunate to have him as a business partner. Like a good captain of a ship he was helping to steer her through troubled water.

With the interest in their cooking school though she was confident they would be able to trade their way out of the financial mess left behind by her late uncle. Of course she couldn't blame him for it as he had got old and in poor health for the last five years of his life. Sadly, the finances of the castle had become an afterthought.

As Meg had kept reminding her, it was a good thing that she came along when she did. And that she was able to go into business with Hunter, otherwise things would have only gotten worse financially.

Looking over the reports and figures Meg had prepared she reasoned that it would take them another twelve to eighteen months to get the books balanced. What they needed was a big publicity event to attract interest in the cooking school from further afield.

Hunter's idea of the worlds largest tea party might just do the trick she thought. She made a note to spend some time with him to go over the idea in more detail.

It wasn't just his good looks and delicious food she thought to herself. It was his business savvy as well that led her to enjoy his company.

Her train of thought was interrupted by Woolsworth.

'Ma'am I forgot to mention earlier,' Woolsworth said.

'Yes Woolsworth?'

'A Janet Brown called for you earlier. While you were busy with the Constable. I didn't want to disturb you then and suggested you would call her back.'

'Very good, thank you.'

She went for her phone book to find her number. Woolsworth stood waiting at the door as she searched. The phone book didn't appear to have her number. She wondered if she might be able to Google it up like Meg would.

Woolsworth cleared his throat to get her attention.

She turned back around to find he had his hand outstretched with a slip of paper in it.

'The phone number Ma'am!'

'Oh thanks ever so much Woolsworth,' she replied taking the note from him.

She waited until he headed off before dialing the number.

Janet answered on the second ring.

'Janet Brown Dressmakers, how can I help you?'

'Oh Janet, it's Susie Carter here returning your call,' she said.

They spent a moment exchanging pleasantries.

'I heard you had some dramas earlier today with those Americans?' Janet asked.

Susie smiled to herself at how quickly word had got around town and beyond. It was one of those charming characteristics of the area. Virtually nothing can be kept a secret long, especially a drama involving police, guns, Americans and local farmers.

For the next five minutes Susie gave her a detailed account of the events at the Smugglers Inn. She told them how terrified they all were as they were bundled into the car at gun point and driven in the direction of the Foley residence. Only to be held up by old farmer Harrison whose old truck loaded with hay bales just decided to stop right there and then. Susie sung the praises of the Inspector and Constable Daniels recalling how brave and gallant they both were.

Janet listened on fascinated stopping now and then to ask questions.

'So do you think they committed the murder then?' She asked fascinated by it all.

'It seems likely. At this stage though I am not sure if there is enough evidence to put them at the scene of the crime. Constable Daniels suggest that they were hopeful of getting a confession from them, otherwise they would need to find more solid evidence against them before they could charge them with murder.'

'Well they have a stronger motive than anyone so far!' Janet added.

'Indeed they did, and the fact they came all the way from LA to collect the money owed to them demonstrates how much motivation they did have.'

'Yes you are right,' Janet agreed. 'Well let's hope that they are the ones and we can put the whole mess behind us!'

'You know I was just thinking the same thing earlier,' Susie replied, and they both chuckled. For a moment Susie thought how nice it was to have a local friend around her age that she found so easy agreeable to chat with. She decided it was probably worth taking more time to get to know Janet.

'Oh really, great minds and all that,' Janet responded. They both laughed some more.

'Now dear, what was it you called me about?'

Janet explained that she was in Polmerton earlier in the day and drove past the harbour. Because of the storm the other night she wondered if it had cleared some sand away from the cave entrance. Given Susie's interest in all things Smugglers and the like she stopped by to have a look.

'So I just wanted to let you know,' Janet said.

'Oh go on then?'

'Well I was right in my thinking. The storm has washed away most of the sand and opened up the top of the cave mouth. You might need to do a bit of digging but if you were ever going to poke around and have a look, now would be the time.'

'Oh yes what a good idea, it hadn't occurred to me!'

'Only reason I thought of it was because when the historical society found it last time, you know with the picture in the local paper and all.'

'Yes I remember?'

'Well that was the day after a big storm like the one we just had.'

Janet explained that with a bit of digging away the sand around the mouth of the cave you could squeeze through the entrance. Once inside though it opened up into a nice big area that a shortish person could stand up in.

They both laughed at the idea when they realised they were both on the shortish side.

'Short and I am afraid getting a little to round,' Susie laughed.

'Oh that would be all those treats Mr McGill is feeding you up on!' Janet said.

They both roared with laughter at the idea.

'So now I know his master plan,' teased Susie, 'he is trying to fatten me up for market!' More laughter followed. Susie made up her mind she was definitely going to continue the friendship with Janet as she was enjoying the conversation so much. No one could ever replace the special bond she had with Margery as they grew up together from a very young age, but it would be nice to have another friend more local.

Janet said she had to go as she had a customer coming for a fitting shortly. Before she went, she told Susie to be careful if she did go in the cave. The oceans were very changeable at the moment and the high tide could come in quicker than expected.

'Oh dear yes I best look into that.'

'Yes only go in if it is the low tide mark and take someone with you if you do!'

With that they said their good byes.

Susie hung up the phone feeling rather pleased.

The idea of a new friend in the area delighted her. And the thrill of exploring caves and smugglers tunnels reignited her adventurous spirit from her youth.

She decided to spend the rest of the evening reading more of the 'Smugglers Guide to Cornwall.'

33

The next morning after a sound sleep Susie and Max headed into the woods and up the hill. Max was in his element as he chased birds and a couple of squirrels. They worked their way up the long winding path until it opened up at the top.

Out of breath Susie took a seat on a rocky ledge. From there the view was spectacular. The storm clouds from the last week had all but cleared leaving blue skies and the promise of sunshine to come later in the day.

It had taken her some time to get to sleep. With the fright they all had at the hands of the Americans she reasoned it was no wonder. But what had her really awake was reading the book about the smugglers of the Cornwall area. The stories fascinated and captivated her. Previously she thought she wouldn't have taken a lot of interest in such things. But now living in Ash Castle and feeling more a part of the community every day she found the history of the area exciting.

She wondered if she might speak with Janet about joining the historical society. No doubt being a non-profit community group they could probably use all the help they could get. It might make a good social outlet she told Max as she threw a stick for him.

Max bounded after the stick and skidded down the hill and into the bushes.

For a moment all she could see was bushes moving about before he appeared again with a stick in mouth. He ran up to her with his tail wagging about like crazy.

'Come here dear boy,' she said, 'Your snout is covered in cob webs!'

He placed his snout on her knee so she could pick the cobwebs away.

When he least expected it she grabbed the stick and tossed it out into a clearing. He barked with delight and headed after it.

After returning to the castle Susie showered and dressed. She had a hearty breakfast of English Muffins with jam and a strong coffee. Feeling happy that she had a good start to the day, she headed into town.

After some thought she had decided she wanted to visit Patty Malone. Firstly to see if all was okay after what took place with the Americans the day before. And secondly she wanted to see if she could find out more details about the smuggler tunnel that led out from the old unsued cellar.

Things were quieter than usual at the Smugglers Inn when she arrived. It was a good opportunity for a catch up with Patty when she was not too busy. They chatted some more about the arrest of the two Americans and discussed the possibility that they may have been responsible for the murder of Mr Foley.

'Do you think they will be charging them with the murder then?' Patty asked.

'Oh I suspect so,' Susie replied, 'it seems obvious that they did it.'

'Oh yes, and poor Mandy might have been next if it wasn't for you and Meg acting so fast.'

'Never moved so fast in all my life,' Susie joked. They both laughed at the idea of them racing off to tackle armed intruders.

'Well the important thing is everyone was safe in the end.'

Susie agreed. They had all been very lucky that no one had been injured or worse. She had no doubt they meant business. It was a lot of money they aimed to collect and they knew that it would have been impossible for them to collect it from abroad. She was certain they would have gone to any lengths possible to get the money they felt was owed to them. A strong motive like money made them all the more dangerous.

Patty excused herself for a moment while she went to take delivery of snacks. Susie could hear her out in the storage room giving instructions to the driver on where to stack up the boxes she had ordered.

Susie took the opportunity to look at the old photos of the town that lined the walls of the Inn. The Smugglers Inn was like a time machine. When you stepped inside, you literally went back in time through the history of Polmerton and the surrounding area. It was no wonder the historical society held their monthly meetings here.

The old black and white photos from many years ago showed the faces of salty sea dogs, and miners. Tin mines had littered the hills behind Polmerton and the area thrived because of them. With the mines long since closed the ancestors of many of the miners still wore the hardship of a life in the mines on their faces. She noticed that they all seemed shorter and smaller overall back then. Probably needed to be to get in and out of the mines she decided.

Old photos of the main street showed the development of the town over the last one hundred years or so. The street was largely unchanged in that time except for some more modern retail shops at the southern end of the street. They were past the old town and past the harbour with its bobbing boats.

In recent times development plans for new townhouses around the back of the harbour had been put forward, but Susie and many others felt that they were not really in keeping with the village itself.

'Aye, some great shots of the old town hey?' Patty asked joining Susie.

'There certainly are indeed!'

'Shame that photography only goes back so far though.'

'Yes, imagine if we had photos of the town from two hundred years ago?'

'Now there would be some stories to tell,' Patty laughed and headed back to the bar.

She poured herself a sparkling mineral water with a squeeze of lemon in it. She offered Susie a drink but Susie said she was fine for the moment. Down at the end of the bar Susie pulled out a bar stool and took a seat. Patty joined her at the end and they chatted some more.

'Oh I am thinking of joining the historical society,' Susie informed her.

'Oh do, yes!' Patty said delighted. Patty explained that currently it was only her and Janet that made up the female representation on the society. The rest were largely stuffy old men who would soon be considered historical themselves. They both laughed. Patty said she always put on a good spread of food for them when they had their meetings.

'Actually I wanted to ask you Patty,' Susie said cautiously. She had taken Janet's warning that Patty was reluctant to let too many people know about the smugglers tunnel and would deny its existence.

'What's that then?'

'Well I have been reading the book 'Smugglers History of Cornwall',' Susie replied.

'Oh aye, a popular book no doubt!'

'Yes well in it there is a paragraph,'

'About the hidden treasure in a Smugglers tunnel?' Patty cut her off with a big belly laugh.

Not sure how to take her comment Susie blushed.

Patty explained to her that she had a blanket policy of denying the existence of a smugglers tunnel from the Inn. For years since that book came out she had people come from all over the world in search of the supposed hidden treasure.

'If there were such a tunnel, it would be full of dangers,' Patty said.

'Yes I am sure.'

'So I just tell people it was all an urban myth, you know it's easier that way!'

'I can imagine so, yes,' Susie said sounding disappointed.

'Oh now, no need for the long face,' Patty teased her.

The truth was Susie had become fascinated with the idea of smugglers and the old history of the town. The very idea that there might have been a tunnel to the Inn was an exciting prospect she had thought. In her mind it somehow validated the town as a true part of the history of Cornwall.

Patty leaned in closer to Susie across the bar. She beckoned to Susie to do the same. And then she whispered in her ear.

'There is indeed such a tunnel, but the book got it wrong.'

'You don't say?'

'Oh yes, but it's a secret you see!'

'But what about the news article, with the photo of the historical society and all?' Susie asked confused.

'Got it wrong!'

'They did what?' Susie was no baffled.

'The article suggested the tunnel started in the cellar of the Inn,' Patty explained, 'the one from out the back of the old theatre room.'

'Yes that was my understanding of it,' Susie agreed.

'Well that was wrong wasn't it?'

Patty led Susie outside and showed her the lay of the land behind the Inn. She pointed out the extension of the theatre room to the back of the Inn and explained that based on the fall of the land it would have been impossible for the tunnel to have reached that far back.

Susie was no engineer, but having it pointed out to her it made total sense.

She followed Patty back into the bar disappointed.

'So there is no tunnel then?' Susie sighed.

'Oh there is a tunnel but not in the location the newspaper said!'

'What? Well where is it then?' Susie asked with confusion sounding in her voice.

Patty again motioned for Susie to follow her. They walked towards the front of the Inn. There in the entrance hall at the bottom of the steps leading in, was an old cupboard to hang your coats in during winter. It was mostly only used by the locals and the cupboard was rarely opened. Patty opened the door and pointed in.

Susie poked her head in and looked. She couldn't see anything out of the ordinary. She looked back at Patty confused.

'Look at this!' Patty said. She pushed on one corner of the floor of the cupboard. There was an old pair of boots, and several umbrellas mostly discarded on the floor. She pulled everything out and pressed harder on the corner. Then a clicking sound was heard as the latch released its grip.

'Stand back then,' she instructed Susie, as much for dramatic effect as anything.

The flooring lifted up, and she pulled it out of the cupboard. It revealed the opening to what indeed looked like a tunnel. There was a narrow shaft lined with brick and bluestone. A small wooden ladder led down to the pit at the bottom. In the pit there appeared to be an opening which led towards the street in the direction of the police station.

'Oh my!' Susie gasped.

'Oh, aye!'

Patty reconstructed the cupboard floor and returned the boots and umbrellas to their place before they were disturbed.

'Well I never expected it to be here in the front of the Inn,' Susie said a little disappointed. 'I really thought it would have gone to the cellar at the back.'

'No one does, but it makes sense when you think about it. Why tunnel further past the front of the Inn if you don't need to?'

'I guess so,' Susie agreed. 'Well I guess that explains why Constable Daniels couldn't locate a tunnel when he searched the old cellar.'

Patty informed her that there is an opening at the back of the cellar that some had confused as the tunnel. But it only went in a few feet. It might have once been an attempt to start a tunnel however it didn't get far.

Susie had a look of disappointment on her face. Patty asked her why she looked so deflated about the location of the tunnel. In the back of Susie's mind, she had told Patty, was the idea that whoever fired the fatal shot at Mr Foley that night, might have escaped through the smugglers tunnel. With all the confusion of the moment they could have just gone back stage, down into the cellar and out through the tunnel.

'Oh I see where you are coming from now,' Patty said nodding her head.

'Seems unlikely they used the tunnel now though,' Susie laughed, 'they would have been better off going out through the front door.'

Patty joined her in laughter. She agreed that it would have been easier just to walk right out, rather than go to the trouble of opening the tunnel trap door, and making sure it was returned in its proper place.

'Besides, judging by the amount of dust lying around it didn't look as though anyone had been in there for some years!' Susie said.

34

Susie bid farewell to Patty and thanked her for her time. She left the Inn and could see Hunter waving from across the road. She went over to see him and was greeted by a lovely bunch of flowers.

'Oh heavens, what are these for?' she asked with surprise.

'I just picked them from my garden and I thought they were just your colours,' Hunter said.

Susie breathed in the aroma coming from the beautiful arrangement of flowers. They were indeed her colours with lovely shades of lilacs and yellows. Nice soft pastel colours had always been her favourite. She had dabbled with watercolours for a few years as she loved the subtle soft effects you could achieve with them. The flowers reminded her that she had intended to take up painting again.

'Well thank you so much,' Susie smiled. She gave Hunter a hug and kissed him on the cheek. It was a kind gesture, and she considered him to be very thoughtful.

'Do you have time for a cup of tea then?' he asked.

She checked her watch. She wanted to get back to the castle soon and rally Meg to her coming adventure. But it was such a lovely, thoughtful thing of him to do she couldn't possibly refuse a cup of tea with him.

'Oh I have some news I do,' Hunter said as he led her out to the courtyard behind the bakery. To get there she had to follow him through the bakery, and out through the kitchen. The rear door opened up to the courtyard.

Every time Susie came into the courtyard area she marvelled at what a terrific job he had done with renovating it all. Behind the shop and around the permitter of the courtyard were old stables he had converted into his home.

They sat down and Hunter poured her a cup of tea. He already had one on the go but he topped it up, anyway.

'Now, what's your news?'

'Well I just bumped into Constable Daniels,'

'Oh what did he have to say?'

She was all ears as Hunter updated her on the conversation. The Constable had told him that they were unable to charge the two Americans with the murder of James Foley. The reason being that they hadn't entered the country at the time of the murder. According to their passports they entered the day after the incident occurred.

'Oh no, that's a shame really!' Susie replied.

'It's not all lost though,' Hunter continued. He told her that they were still going to be charged with serious offences of kidnapping and threatening harm with a deadly weapon and all.

Hunter went on to tell her the rest of the story. After conducting a number of international database searches it turned out the pair were wanted in the United States on a string of similar offences.

He said that under the International Treaty Agreement they would have to extradite the pair of them back to LA where they would face a court. They were most likely facing thirty to forty years each for the string of crimes they had committed. He finished up sharing the story by adding that crime still doesn't pay.

They both laughed at the idea.

'That leaves us still with one major problem!' Susie sighed.

'Oh aye, what is that then love?'

Susie took a sip of her tea.

Her mind raced as she went through all the information she had to date. It was clearly not Mr Lightfoot as the gun he had wasn't the gun that fired the fatal shot. Now it appeared it was not the two Americans as they were not in the country at the time. She considered that if they had been, then they would probably be charged with the murder. There was no doubting that they had the strongest motive of all.

Her face went blank. She was at a loss then to figure out who it might be.

'You okay there?' Hunter asked.

'Yes, well, no not really!'

'Well what is it then?'

'The murderer! They are still at large!'

With that Susie stood up and told Hunter she must dash off. She gave him another quick peck on the cheek, took her flowers and headed out the door.

Susie turned right and headed the couple of doors up the street and into the police station. She found both the Inspector and the Constable standing staring at a wall. Their backs were to her and they were deep in thought and conversation. So much so they didn't even hear her enter.

She coughed loudly to announce her arrival. Still, they didn't hear her.

'Excuse me officers!' she said rather firmly.

It startled them both. They swung around to see who had interrupted their discussion.

'Lady Carter,' the Inspector nodded, 'to what do we owe the pleasure?'

'I've come to see what progress is being made on catching the killer?'

'The young Constable has come up with a fine idea,' the Inspector said. He told Susie that the lad had been watching an episode of Murder Method when he noticed the detectives used a large white board. On it they put a photo of each of the suspects in the case to give them a visual representation on the situation.

Susie stepped forward to see what they had been looking at.

She was impressed. It seems they had been busy. Right there on the wall of the Polmerton Police Station there was evidence of some serious police work finally taking place.

The Constable had managed to secure photos of all the suspects in the murder of James Foley. He had them all pinned up on the wall. Under each photo was the name of the person, and details about motive, means and other relevant information.

In all a total of about nine main suspects.

Susie scanned through the faces.

Karl Lightfoot was at the top of the list.
Patty Malone
Mandy Reed
Patrick Johnston
Irvine Maxwell
Cecil Miller
Susie Carter
Janet Brown
Hunter McGill
Frederick Hallow

Susie read through the list at first not fully taking it all in. Then she paused and took a closer look.

Shocked she took a step back and clutched her hands to her chest. It dawned on her that the police were considering her as one of the main suspects.

'Good heavens above!' she declared.

'Now Lady Carter, it's all just routine investigation!' the Inspector assured her.

'Yes I am sure, but surely you don't think?'

'At this stage we are simply sifting through the facts!'

Susie informed them that the fact of the matter was that she had nothing to do with the murder of James Foley and they should promptly remove her name and photo from the board at once.

With that she marched out of the police station.

35

Susie headed back to the castle. There she informed Meg that they would be going on an adventure. She asked Meg to located strong torches and make sure they had fresh batteries in them.

She fetched Max and found his lead. He wagged his tail with great vigour thrusting it from side to side. He was excited to be going on his second walk for the day.

They loaded into the Land Rover and headed back into town. Susie explained all to Meg on the way. She told her about the conversation with Janet, and how there was a fair chance that the storm had washed away the sand blocking the entrance to the cave. Meg squealed with delight at the prospect of going exploring in old caves. She told Susie how much she enjoyed working with her instead of old man Ash.

There was great excitement in the car as they came upon the harbour. Susie found a car spot which was now a lot easier given the tourists had mostly left town.

The car park was to the north of the Harbour. It stood at an elevated position which gave them a terrific view across the harbour with its many sailing boats and brightly coloured larger fishing boats. It was low tide so there was virtually no water at all inside the protective walls of the harbour. All the boats lay to one side patiently waiting on the return of the ocean when the tides changed.

Across the other side of the harbour were a row of delightful sailors cottages. Mostly white, with a few colourful exceptions, they all displayed bursts of colour from the flower baskets along the window sills.

It was postcard perfect view of the town of Polmerton and one that Susie loved. She felt the gentle breeze of the ocean as she fastened the lead to Max's collar. He was happy to sit patiently while she attached the lead.

The smell of salt air and seaside fishing villages greeted them as they made their way down the stairs onto a boardwalk. The boardwalk could be taken north around the small sandy beach to a rather large rocky headland.

As Janet had described it, the cave opening was nestled in to the side of the headland. She had informed them that the cave entrance was not immediately obvious to the casual observer. Part of the reason why it made such an ideal smugglers tunnel in the first place she had suggested. She instructed Susie that she was going to have to think like a smuggler in order locate the cave opening.

In the phone call though she did say that the recent storm was probably going to have revealed the cave opening more than it might normally be. This was the very best opportunity to locate it and if she felt so inclined, to explore it.

A good forty minutes went by as Meg and Susie walked back and forth around the base of the headland. They found a few cracks and crevices but nothing that might constitute an opening to a cave.

Exhausted they sat down on some rocks and took a breather. Max ran up and down the beach chasing sea gulls. He was sure he would get one, but they always managed to avoid his advances at the last minute.

'Well, I am exhausted and we are no closer to finding the jolly cave!' Susie said sounding disappointed.

'Oh I know, so am I,' Meg replied.

'It might have been better if Janet had joined us. At least it would have been quicker to find.'

'I hope she wasn't having a laugh at our expense,' Meg joked.

Susie said she didn't think so. Janet had been excited to tell Susie everything she knew about the cave and didn't think she would joke about its existence. They discussed where they had looked and wondered if they didn't need to go around the headland to the other side to find it.

Max was madly barking off in the distance. He had run up the beach and looked like he was digging.

'He must be chasing a crab the silly fellow,' Meg laughed.

'Oh I hope he doesn't get bitten then.'

They laughed as all they could see was his backside sticking out in the air, his two hind legs, and his tail thumping from side to side. His two front paws were madly working away digging as clouds of sand flew out behind him.

He barked as loud as he could as the sand flew.

Susie and Meg laughed. Then all of a sudden their laughter was cut short. He just disappeared. Susie gasped. Meg looked at Susie with a look of horror on her face.

They both ran to where they had last seen him. There was a pile of sand where he had been a moment before, and paw marks everywhere, but no sign of Max himself.

'Max!' Susie yelled as loud as she could while running to the spot.

'Max, come here Maxy!' Meg joined in.

They arrived at the spot with no sign of him. Susie's heart skipped a beat. She couldn't stand it if anything happened to her dear beloved Max. She clutched her hands to her chest in astonishment.

'Max!' she called again not knowing where to look to find him.

'Oh my,' Meg said under her breath in disbelief.

Max was gone. He just disappeared.

'We must call someone for help!' Susie yelled.

'Max, here boy!' Meg tried again.

Then quite unexpectedly a pile of sand where he had been digging began to move. At first they thought it might have been a giant crab in the sand until they saw a nose break through. The nose was followed by a snout and then two big brown eyes.

Finally Max pushed his whole head through the sand and shook. The sand in his eyes went flying out, and he barked with delight.

'Oh goodness you gave me such a fright!' Susie said. Max pushed himself through the sand and back into the light of day. He shook his body covering both Susie and Meg in sand and seaweed.

Meg dropped to her knees and hugged the big soggy sandy mess that Max had become. Then her eyes shifted to the hole he had come out of.

'Max I don't believe it!' she said.

'What is it?' Susie asked as she wiped sand off of Max's snout and from around his eyes and ears.

'I think Max just discovered what we have been looking for!' Meg said with an air of disbelief in her tone. 'Quick hand me the torch!'

Susie took the torch out of her jacket pocket and handed it to Meg.

She was down on all fours and with the torch in hand she tried to squeeze herself into the opening. It wasn't quite large enough, so she dropped the torch and shoveled sand out of the way with her hands.

Then she resumed with the torch in hand to push her upper body into the opening.

'Oh my!' she said in a muffled voice.

'What is it dear?' Susie asked. Susie now had a similar view of the back of Meg as they had earlier of the back of Max.

'I think he found it all right!' she said as she pulled herself back out of the hole.

'What?'

'It's the cave entrance!'

36

Susie joined Meg on all fours and they both shoveled more sand out of the way. When the opening was made large enough, they exchanged looks. It was a look of excitement and adventure shared between two friends. The look dared each other to explore and take a chance.

Meg climbed in through the opening first. Once inside Susie went next. Meg had turned around to help her through the opening. The hole they had made in the sand was still a tight fit but once Susie had her torso through, she could see it opened up into a small rocky opening.

'There is an opening over here,' Meg said as she crawled on her hands and knees. Susie followed her and Max wedged himself in between them. On hands and knees they crawled towards the opening Meg had spotted.

It was another tight squeeze through the rocks.

Susie waited while Meg went through this second opening. As Janet had described it to her this was the real cave entrance. Once through here it opened into a larger area they could practically stand up in. To assist she tried to shine the torch ahead of Meg.

Then Meg disappeared through the opening. Next came a squeal of delight.

'What is it dear?' Susie asked.

'Oh it's bigger than I thought it would be!'

Susie poked her head through the opening and with the aid of the torch she could see what Meg was talking about. Meg was slightly taller than Susie and was standing upright in this larger opening of the cave.

'Just watch these jagged rocks,' Meg instructed her.

Susie eased her way through and it wasn't long before she joined Meg and Max inside the cave. For a moment they both stood there shining the torches around taking in all they could see.

'Can you imagine that a few hundred years ago this would have been full of smuggler loot!' Susie said.

'Never?'

'Well at least temporarily, I am not sure if the tide will come in and fill this little hideout up,' Susie said. She thought back to what Janet had said. She warned her to go at low tide and to be careful of the tides.

The water had seemed far enough away, and it was definitely low tide now so Susie felt they were safe to explore for a few hours.

The cave was damp and had a pungent smell. The kind of smell Susie remembered from her childhood collecting shells of the beach and taking them home. Little did she know the shells were occupied by living creatures who promptly died when being taken from their environment. Her mother had to take them away as the smell had become repulsive. As she now looked around the cave a similar smell filled her nostrils.

'Rotting seaweed,' Meg said. Having lived her whole life in Polmerton, and spending a lot of time at the beach, she had a well tuned nose for the various aromas she would find at the beach.

'Oh it's a little strong isn't it,' Susie laughed.

'Where do you suppose the tunnel might be from here?' Meg asked.

Susie laughed when she told Meg what Janet had said. She had told Susie that once inside the main cave they could locate the entrance to the tunnel behind a large rock. As she said it they both saw the funny side of it. The cave itself was forged from a large rock, and everywhere they looked all they could see was large rocks.

'Well I am no engineer,' Meg said, 'but it makes sense that the tunnel should be towards the town.'

'Yes you are right,' Susie agreed, 'it would need to be on this side as that would be the hill leading back to town.'

They both flashed their torches and decided it could be one of four larger rocks. They went to the first one and looked behind it but there was nothing of interest to see.

They started to move to the next one when Max barked.

Startled they shone their torches in the direction of his bark in time to see him disappear behind a smaller rock in the corner.

'Well that's the last place I would have looked,' Meg said.

'Exactly! That's why it's a good place to put it,' Susie said heading in that direction.

Max was barking to them with excitement. To Susie and Meg the sound of his bark was muffled suggesting he was well into the tunnel.

They arrived at the opening of the tunnel and paused for a moment.

'I think we are going to get a little dirty,' Meg said.

'Well I'm game if you are!'

'Okay lets do it.'

With that Meg pushed herself into the opening of the tunnel. She used her torch out in front of her to light the way. On all fours she worked herself into the tunnel. To her surprise there was more room in the tunnel than she had thought.

Susie followed. She was astonished at how precise the tunnel had been formed. The old tin miners who made these smugglers tunnels were extremely good at their craft. The walls to the tunnel were supported by oak timber beams and they were still as solid as the day they were built.

They climbed on. Ahead they could hear Max stopping to paw at the walls now and then, and to bark at them to see if they were still coming. Right behind you they assured him.

It was mostly an uphill climb which made sense Susie informed Meg. The High Street through Polmerton was a good height in elevation above the sea level. So they were going to have to climb until they reached that point. Then it should level off.

The temperature inside the tunnel was rising as they climbed higher. There was very little in the way of fresh air making its way into the tunnel. The further into the tunnel they went the thinner and staler the air appeared to get.

Finally after about fifteen minutes the tunnel abruptly leveled off and flattened out just as Susie had predicted. The good news was that it also opened out into a small but a wider area. They discussed it being some sort of room where there smugglers could hide out and take a rest. There was a bench seat to one side made out of a solid piece of oak. It was wedged at either end into the rock face.

'Let's take a break,' Meg said, and they both sat on the bench to catch their breath. The rising temperature had caused them both to break out into a sweat.

They sat in silence for a few moments. Max couldn't settle though. There was too much for him to explore. He went on ahead, then returned. He repeated the pattern several times.

It wasn't long before they started to hear muffled voices. At first a deep manly voice with a thick accent, and then a younger man. Meg and Susie looked at each other in shock. They tried their hardest to make the voices out but couldn't hear what they were saying.

'You know, I think we might be right below the police station,' Susie whispered. She told Meg about the map Janet had shown her which showed that part of the tunnel at one stage went to the police station in an attempt to break one of the Carter brothers free from the lock up.

'Oh lets have some fun then,' Meg said cheekily.

'How so?'

'Like this,' Meg replied. 'HELLLOOOO!' she yelled at the top of her voice.

Susie laughed. That was sure to give the Inspector and Constable a mystery to investigate. Hunter had told Susie once that the police station was haunted from ghosts of prisoners past. Maybe the police from years past had become spooked by the sounds of smugglers right below them.

'I don't think they can hear you dear,' Susie said.

'Oh drat!'

They both laughed before deciding to push on.

Ahead Max could be heard barking and digging.

'Now if my memory serves me correctly,' Susie said as they entered the next section of the tunnel, 'we should be going under High street soon.'

'And will that take us into the Smugglers Inn?'

'I suspect so!'

They pushed on for another fifteen minutes. It was slow going, and hard on the knees. Eventually they got to the end of the tunnel.

Meg found the small ladder that led up to the secret entrance inside the Inn.

Susie explained there was no use trying to open the hatch door as it needed to be opened from the other side as Patty had explained to her. Meg asked her what they should do now, and they decided that they should turn around and head back.

As she was at the end Susie tried to turn around to head back towards the small room. It was hot and steamy and the sweat was running down the side of her face. The air was dank, and it was getting harder to breathe. Having suffered from anxiety and fear of small places in the past she now found herself starting to struggle for breath. The anxiety had been kept at bay with the excitement of the adventure, but now as they were attempting to turn around and head out it raised its ugly head.

She panicked as she attempted to turn. Her top got caught on a jagged rock and pulled against her as she tried to move. In a moment of fear she pulled herself hard against the caught top. In one almighty heave she managed to pull the garment free as it ripped. The release of the tension however caused her head to snap forward. It banged against one of the oak timber pillars used to support the walls.

There was a sickening thud as her forehead collided with the timber. It split her forehead open above her eyebrow and instantly knocked her unconscious.

Her body slumped forward motionless.

'Susie?' Meg asked unsure of what just happened.

Meg shone the torch on her and could see the blood running out of the cut and down the side of her face.

The motionless body of Susie Carter was blocking the tunnel. At the point where it went under the road to the Smugglers Inn was where it was at its narrowest. There was no way that Meg could get past Susie.

Max was trapped behind Meg. He could sense something was not right and started to whimper.

Meg managed to half crawl over Susie so she could try to wake her up. She checked her pulse at the side of her neck. There was one which was a relief. She also checked her breathing. Meg was ever grateful for the first aid training she took as a Girl Guide some years ago.

She gently tapped Susie on the side of the face trying to wake her.

'Susie, wake up.' She said.

There was no response.

'Come on Susie,' she tried again.

Again there was no response.

'Oh no, what on earth are we going to do?' she asked of no one.

Max barked. It wasn't one of his happy barks. It was one of concern.

'Help!' she cried out.

Then she paused and waited for a response. None came.

'Help us!' she tried again. Still no response came.

Meg realised it was useless trying to cry for help. They were at that point in the tunnel where they were right under the footpath of the road. It was a busy and noisy part of the town and the chances of anyone hearing them from down there was very slim.

She decided to preserve her energy for the moment. Meg tried to revive Susie again but with no luck.

Tired and frightened she did the one thing she was trying not to do. She fell asleep.

37

Meg had no idea how long she had been asleep for. It could have been five minutes or five hours for all she knew. She was awoken by dreams of crashing waves and rushing water.

Realising where she was and the gravity of their situation her immediate reaction on waking up was to panic. Then she caught herself. She told herself that panicking wasn't going to help anyone.

She paused for a moment and sat quietly.

And that's when she heard it. She could hear the sea making its advance up the beach. The breaking waves were getting closer to the cave entrance. The tides can rise fast around these parts the old fisherman around town would say. Never a slow tide around Cornwall was often quoted when salty sea dogs gathered for an ale at the Smugglers Inn.

Meg knew she didn't have long before the mouth of the cave would be cut off from the rising tide. Maybe an hour, possibly two. She had to get help and get them out of here.

Her train of thought was broken by the sound of a muffled voice. It sounded like it was calling to her. She wasn't sure. With the torch turned off she had been sitting in the dark. She was tired and dehydrated in the heat. For a moment she thought she may have even been getting a little delirious.

But then she heard it again.

It sounded like a voice in the distance calling her. A muffled sound yet a familiar one. A voice she recognised but at the moment she couldn't place it.

Then she thought she saw a flash of light. Just a flicker. But it broke the darkness. Briefly, only for a moment, but she was sure she saw it.

'Help us!' she cried out. Then she paused and sat in silence waiting for a reply.

Nothing came.

Saddened she thought she must have imagined it. Maybe she was dreaming she thought to herself. Maybe there was no voice, no sound. It was all just in her head. Could she be so delirious as to imagine hearing voices?

She felt exhausted and lay back down.

Meg closed her eyes and allowed the wave of sleep to wash over her again. There was no point resisting it. She started to drift off.

Then she heard it again. A muffled sound. It sounded like someone calling to her.

This time she was certain of it.

'Help us!' she cried at the top of her voice.

Max stirred at the sound of her cry. He stretched and got to his feet and came and nuzzled his snout into Meg.

She tried again, 'Help us please!'. She screamed at the top of her voice straining the muscles in the side of her neck.

Max barked to help her.

Again she waited for a response. A brief pause and sure enough she heard a muffled response. She couldn't make out what the voice was saying, but she felt relieved that they were going to be rescued.

The sounds of the crashing waves echoed up the tunnel to them. Meg tried to calculate how long they had been in the tunnel for, and therefore how high the tide had risen, but in her state she was unable to do the maths.

Judging by the increasing volume of the waves though she knew they were getting closer to the cave entrance which would mean they would remain trapped if they didn't get help soon.

Susie started to stir awake. All the shouting by Meg and Max barking had finally helped her come to. Relieved Meg hugged her and tried to help her to sit upright. She told Meg she was dizzy and felt it best if she laid back down. Meg told her help would be there soon.

Meg was so preoccupied with looking after Susie that she almost didn't hear the voice. This time it was less muffled. Previously the voice sounded like it was coming from outside the tunnel, now it sounded like the voice was coming from within the tunnel.

'Help, we are in here!' Meg yelled with delight.

'Okay, stay right there! I am coming to you,' the voice replied.

Meg reassured Susie that they would be rescued shortly.

A few moments later Meg was greeted by a big smiling face as it came around the corner. Constable Daniels had sand on his face and a bead of sweat running across his forehead from the heat. Yet he still managed to bring a smile as he crawled along on all fours.

'Constable Daniels!' Meg squealed with delight. 'Am I ever so glad to see you.'

Ten minutes later they were all safely back in the cave. Constable Daniels had dragged Susie out of the tunnel working backwards on his knees. It was a slow process, but they got there in the end.

'How did you know where to find us?' Meg asked gazing into his big blue eyes once they were all safe.

Constable Daniels told them that a couple of local kids had seen them go into the cave, and when they didn't come out for a few hours, they told their mum. Concerned that the tide was coming in fast she told the police. The Inspector thought nothing of it but sent Daniels down for a look.

'Then I found this,' he said holding up a handkerchief with the letter M stitched on it. He said he found it at the mouth of the cave. Meg thought she must have dropped it accidentally when they were digging out the sand.

'Right we best be getting a move on then,' Constable Daniels said, 'that tide is only fifteen minutes from flooding the cave here.'

Constable Daniels led the way out. He was followed by Susie who had to be helped out. She was still a little unsure on her feet and Meg wondered if she wasn't concussed at all. Meg came out last. The edge of the water was lapping at the soles of Constable Daniels feet as they all gathered on the sand.

'Where is Max?' Meg asked looking around.

'Max!' Constable Daniels called out.

Then they heard Max barking like crazy. He was still inside the cave.

Meg raced over to the opening in the sand and peered inside. Max was barking and madly digging at the sand.

'Max come here boy!' Meg called.

Max was too pre-occupied. Something had his attention, and he was going to unearth it.

Meg pushed back through the opening and down into the cave to see what he was up to. Max continued to bark and dig.

Then she saw it. At first it was just the edge. It looked like an old bag. Perhaps something wrapped up in an old bag. Meg helped Max unearth it brushing the sand away.

Carefully she lifted it out from its position wedged behind some rocks. It was long and narrow and wrapped in the old bag.

'What is it?' Constable Daniels called to her.

'I don't know, here take it!'

She handed it to Daniels through the cave entrance. He placed it on the sand and helped her out. Then he called Max who came bounding out satisfied with his efforts. His tongue hung to one side as he went to see if Susie was okay.

Constable Daniels pulled aside the old bag.

'Oh my!' Meg exclaimed on seeing the contents.

'Goodness me!' Susie joined her in shock.

It was the last thing any of them had expected.

But there it was.

Constable Daniels picked it up and looked at it.

In his hands he held a hunting rifle that was in good condition. A little sand and seaweed but it looked like it hadn't been in the cave for long at all.

The Constable turned it over to examine the butt of the rifle.

And that's when they all gasped in surprise.

38

On the butt of the rifle was a small badge. It had been hand made, and no doubt presented as a gift at some stage.

The badge had large initials on it which read,

IM

Underneath that in smaller print it read,

'To Irvine, All My Love Cecil!'

'What does it mean?' Meg asked confused.

'Looks like this rifle belongs to Irvine Maxwell!' Susie stated as she pat Max on the back of his head.

'Might have just found the murder weapon then!' Constable Daniels replied. He carefully wrapped the rifle back up in the old bag.

Susie suggested they best not jump to any conclusions. She advised them that this was going to need to be examined by forensics to see if there is a match for the bullet that delivered the fatal blow. Until then they shouldn't make any assumptions.

Both agreed. They decided to head straight back to the police station.

'I don't understand,' Meg said sounding confused, 'why would Mr Maxwell want to kill Mr Foley? I thought they were good friends?'

'Well we don't know that it was Mr Maxwell!' Susie stated firmly.

'Yes, it could have just as easily been Cecil Miller!' Constable Daniels agreed. 'They both had good reasons in the end, so either one of them might have done it!'

Susie shook her head with concern. It worried her that Constable Daniels was starting to pick up the worst traits of the Inspector. In particular the trait of jumping to conclusions. It almost cost her Hunter a lengthy prison sentence when the Mayor was murdered. And they turned out to be wrong with their assumption.

Back at the police station they found the Inspector looking extremely relaxed. He had his feet up on the desk and he was busy pushing a cream bun into his mouth. As the door opened, he looked up with a look of guilty pleasure on his face.

'Hello, have a look at you lot,' he laughed as he swallowed the bun. Cream was stuck in the corner of his mouth.

'Have a look at this then!' Constable Daniels said and laid the rifle on a large bench at the back of the office area.

'What have we got here then?'

'Looks like the murder weapon,' the Constable informed him. 'Max and the girls found it in the cave entrance to the old tunnel.'

The Inspectors face lit up with delight. He agreed that it did indeed look like the sort of rifle described to them by the forensics team. Constable Daniels pointed out the badge with the initials.

A smug look came across the face of the Inspector. He folded his arms behind his broad back and walked over to the wall of suspects. Susie watched as the Constable joined him.

With a solid bony finger he jabbed it into the picture of Irvine Maxwell.

'Looks like we have our killer then!' he declared loud enough for all to hear.

'Yes we have,' agreed the Constable. He then jabbed his finger into the photo of Cecil Miller and added, 'or it could be Mr Miller!'

Susie was furious. She expressed her concern about jumping to conclusions too soon. The response from the Inspector was a simple shrug of his shoulders, which upset her even more. Susie marched over to the wall of photos and ripped the picture of her off the wall.

'Well you won't need this any more if you already have your man!' she snorted at them.

'Now Lady Carter, I've warned you in the past about meddling in police matters.' The inspector said to her. He knew he was playing with fire but he was feeling rather pleased with himself for having cracked the case wide open.

The Inspector told the Constable that he was going to deliver the rifle personally to forensics for a thorough examination. He added that the result was obvious and the forensics team would find that this was the rifle that killed Mr Foley.

He then instructed the Constable to go and collect Mr Maxwell and Mr Miller and bring them to the police station for questioning. He suggested putting them both in the lock up to soften them up a bit. An old trick for getting a confession out of a killer that he was confident would work just fine with these two.

'They shouldn't give you too much trouble lad,' the Inspector said, 'and if they do just pull out your baton and give them a good walloping.'

Susie ushered Meg and Max out the door to leave them to do their proper police work. She was concerned about the nature of the Inspectors approach but she realised there wasn't much she could do about it.

39

Meg & Susie made it back to the castle in time to clean up and make plans. They were both exhausted from their big adventure. Susie assured Meg that her lump on her head was not nearly as bad as it looked.

Woolsworth had taken Max out the back to have a hot soapy bath. He insisted the beast was not to come into the house with his sandy paws. Woolsworth had only just finished mopping the floors and the last thing he wanted was sandy paws everywhere. Susie suspected that deep down he was growing rather fond of Max.

Their timing was perfect as the Aunties car was coming up the driveway when Susie came down the stairs. Meg was already busy making a large pot of tea. There was a tray of Cornish delights for them to enjoy.

'Mr McGill must have dropped these off earlier,' Meg said showing the tray to Susie.

It wasn't long before Susie, Meg, Mable & Mildred were all seated in the rotunda among the gardens. The Aunties commented on what a fine job Susie was doing in the garden. It was bringing the place to new life they said.

Susie and Meg took great delight in updating the Aunties with all the news of their explorations of the Smugglers Inn.

'Oh I dare say you two are quite the adventurers,' Mable said.

'Yes, rather daring too,' Mildred agreed.

'But how did you come to know about the tunnel?' Mable asked.

Susie explained that when they last visited, they had dropped off the old books. One of them on the Smugglers History of Cornwall. She read it and it sparked her interest in the history of the area.

She told them how she had visited Acton Castle and learned all about the history of the Carter brothers and other famous smugglers of the area.

And she let them know about the visit she had with Janet Brown to find out more about the possibility of their being smugglers tunnels from the Smugglers Inn. She thought it might have been an angle to explore in the murder of Mr Foley. Perhaps, she suggested, the murderer might have used such a tunnel to escape the scene of the crime. She went on to explain that the location of the tunnel entrance in the Smugglers Inn would have made it impossible.

'Oh Janet will be happy now,' Mable said to Mildred.

'Oh yes, she can rest easy now!' Mildred agreed.

'Why is that then?' Susie asked.

'Well haven't you heard?' Mable asked.

'No?' both Susie and Meg said together.

Mable and Mildred shared the story that they had just heard themselves. The Inspector and Constable had taken Irvine Maxwell into custody. Apparently, they went on, the Inspector located the missing murder weapon which led him right to the door of Mr Maxwell.

'You don't say?' Susie asked. She exchanged a look with Meg which went unnoticed by the Aunties.

'Oh yes, they have cracked the case wide open just now!' Mildred stated confidently.

'But why would Ms Brown be happy about that?' Meg asked confused.

'You don't know?' Mabel asked.

Meg shook her head indicating that she didn't know.

The Aunties took delight in filling in the details. Apparently, or so they had heard, at one time in the past Mr Foley and Ms Brown were rather close. Plans were in place to get married.

'Really?' Susie said with surprise.

'Oh yes, they were often seen around town as a couple you know!' Mable said.

'Yes she was very sad when it all ended a year ago,' Mildred added.

They explained that it all ended when Mr Foley started getting close to Irvine Maxwell. That he had left Janet and started a brief liaison with Mr Maxwell. Then a few weeks later he was gone back to Hollywood.

'Oh I had no idea!' Susie said, 'The poor girl must have been heartbroken then.'

'Oh yes, she loved him very much. She had hoped they might reunite this year when he returned.'

'That explains why she threw herself at the body of Mr Foley then,' Meg said.

Meg poured them all fresh cups of tea. The tray that had been dropped off by Hunter earlier was going down a treat. It was a selection of his fluffy delicious scones with local jam and cream, and his Cornish jam shortbreads. And he had added in for good measure his new treat the Australian Lamington.

'Yes the poor girl has been very sad by it all,' Mildred said trying a lamington.

'I imagine so,' Susie replied. She decided she must have Janet over soon for afternoon tea. Give the poor love a friendly ear if she needed someone to talk to.

'She will be relieved that the police look like they have the case solved now,' Mabel said.

'Yes very true,' Mildred agreed, 'though I thought it was more likely to have been Cecil Miller if we were honest.'

'Oh yes, it was more likely Cecil. He was the jealous type after all,' Mabel agreed.

'Mind you, I'm surprised it wasn't the daughter!' Mildred said boldly.

'Good heavens,' Susie said almost choking on her tea, 'do you mean young Mandy?'

'No never!' Meg said shaking her head.

'Well yes she had more reason to do it than anyone!' Mabel said.

Mildred and Mabel spent the next few minutes informing them of the shocking upbringing the poor girl had to endure. There was talk of him interfering with her as a child, and with all the money problems he had caused. They had thought it was her all along.

'Mind you,' Mabel said after thinking about it, 'I still think Mr Lightfoot probably wanted to do it more than anyone!'

'Oh yes you are right!' Mildred agreed.

Meg and Susie exchanged looks. They both had the idea that it might be time to wrap up the tea party as soon as possible.

'Well anyone could have done it!' Susie said trying to wind the conversation up.

'Are you sure it wasn't those Americans dear?' Mabel asked Susie.

'Oh that was a messy business wasn't it?' Mildred said to Mabel. They nodded in unison to each other.

Susie stood up and declared she thought she might need to lay down for a while.

Her head was starting to spin.

The Aunties agreed she should as she was looking pale.

They bid each other farewell.

40

Susie had been taking a nap for a few hours when she heard the car come up the driveway. She got up off the bed and went out on to the balcony to see who it was. A gentle breeze kissed her cheeks, and she felt refreshed and alive again.

Max joined her on the balcony. He stood against her leg and rubbed his head against her. She patted him behind the ears as she watched Constable Daniels park the police car in the parking space.

Good timing she thought to herself. She was keen to hear an update on what had transpired with Irvine & Cecil.

She had been trying not to draw any conclusions herself, but the rifle did indicate that one of them may have been involved. But which one. That was the question that was troubling her when she laid down. Now that she was up she decided that it was more likely to have been Cecil. He had declared on a number of occasions that he would have done it given half a chance. An admission that perhaps was a cry for help she wondered.

He definitely had the jealous personality trait that might lead one to take such drastic action. And Irvine & James had given him a reason to be jealous. The affair between them regardless of how brief it was may have been reason enough. Throw in the loan of the money, and the fact that Foley was always putting Cecil down for no apparent reason. Well all of that made more sense to her than Irvine Maxwell doing it.

Yet the Aunties had heard the word that it was Mr Maxwell who was under the spotlight of the law for the moment.

Now that Constable Daniels was here she could get some clarity on the matter.

She found Meg and Constable Daniels sitting in the lounge chatting. They were seated on the same sofa and looked very cosy together. He had showered and changed into a fresh uniform after having crawled through the tunnel to rescue them earlier.

Susie greeted him with a big hug and thanked him for being so heroic.

'All in a days work Lady Carter!' he said as his cheeks flushed red with embarrassment.

He told Susie what he had just been telling Meg.

The Inspector had arrived back from the forensics department and had questioned both Maxwell and Miller in the station. They had been in the lock up for a good hour as per the instructions. Constable Daniels didn't really think it did much to soften them up for a confession though as they were both adamant they had nothing to do with it.

After an hour of interviewing them both the Inspector had decided to release Mr Miller. He held Irvine Maxwell in the lock up pending charging him with the murder of James Foley the next day.

'Why the next day?' Susie asked. She was shocked by the news but she assumed that if the Inspector had questioned them for an hour, then something must have been unearthed.

'Oh, forensics have told him they would have a match with the bullet and the rifle by midday tomorrow.' Constable Daniels said.

'I see, so if the bullet matches the rifle then he plans to charge Mr Maxwell with murder then?'

'Yes that about sums it all up!' Constable Daniels agreed.

Susie asked Daniels what new information had come to light. He informed her that mostly the discussion was around money loaned to Mr Foley. Apparently the total of the loans made to Mr Foley where closer to seventy five thousand pounds. Susie was shocked to hear it was that high and wondered why they didn't tell her the full picture earlier. It occurred to her that perhaps that might be an indication of their guilt so they kept it quiet.

The Constable explained that Mr Maxwell had admitted to some heated exchanges in the lead up to the opening night with Mr Foley.

Maxwell wanted all the money returned as he and Mr Miller needed to undertake some urgent repairs to their property.

At one stage, according to Mr Maxwell, Foley had turned up at their home drunk and threatened to beat up Mr Miller. Maxwell had taken great offence and a shouting match soon escalated into a punch up. Irvine Maxwell come out of the fight in a good deal better shape and demanded his money back within a week.

'And Mr Maxwell admitted to all of this?' Susie asked surprised.

'Oh yes,' Constable Daniels said, 'he said he was innocent, and he had nothing to hide in the matter. So he was quite prepared to share every last detail of his relationship with Mr Foley.'

'Good heavens!' Susie exclaimed.

'Sounds like he might need a good lawyer,' Meg replied.

'Oh aye, he has a friend in London who is a Barrister. He is driving down first thing tomorrow morning to take up the case!'

41

Susie awoke the next morning after a restless night sleep. She had tossed and turned, her mind full of possibilities around who the real murderer might be. Despite the evidence now stacking up against Irvine she still felt something about it all didn't add up.

Constable Daniels had stayed for dinner which she was happy about. She had decided to make herself scarce though to give Meg and him some space. Sometimes you need to have fertile soil to let love blossom was a favourite saying of her mothers.

She had sat at the small dining table in the kitchen. From there she could hear the occasional laughter coming from the lounge. It filled her with joy to see that the two of them were getting on so well. Susie made a mental note to check in with the Inspector to see if he had a chance to talk to Constable Daniels, to give him a nudge along.

Filled with concern for Irvine and Cecil, Susie decided she would go and visit Cecil this morning to see how he was getting on. It must have been a real shock to him to have his life partner accused of murder and locked up. She couldn't imagine how it might feel but she was sure it wasn't a good feeling.

She arrived in Marazion around nine thirty that morning. When she pulled up in the street, she noticed Cecil's car had the boot up. It was a beautiful new black Audi Q5. Cecil was busy loading suitcases into the boot.

How odd Susie thought to herself. She wondered where on earth he would be going at a time like this? For a brief moment she debated if she should go in or not. He did look to be in a hurry. She decided in the end she would just pop in and see if he was okay.

'Hello dear!' she called out as she was coming up the driveway. He seemed deep in thought so she didn't want to startle him.

'Oh, Lady Carter,' he replied, 'you startled me!'

'I'm so sorry Cecil. I just wanted to see if you are okay?'

Cecil assured her that he was. He suggested a nice cup of tea to which Susie readily agreed. Inside Susie sat on a kitchen stool while Cecil put the kettle on and fetched the tea pot.

'I wanted to see if you are feeling okay, with the shock of Irvine being arrested and all?' Susie asked with concern.

'It was a bit of a shock really,' he said, 'but not a surprise!'

'Really? Why wasn't it a surprise?' Susie asked.

Cecil explained that they had both expected the finger of blame to be pointed at Irvine at some stage. Given his relationship with Foley, and the money owed, it was only a matter of time. When the rifle went missing they were sure it would be found and lead to Irvine being arrested. He went on to say that when it happened they had a plan of what they were going to do. Part of that plan was to have their good friend, a Barrister from London, to come and defend Irvine.

'Oh well you have given it some thought then?' Susie asked.

'Very much so. We talked about it a lot. He's innocent though you know!'

Susie shook her head in agreement. She wasn't sure what to think any more. It was clear that someone pulled the trigger. What wasn't clear to her was who and why?

'Yes I am sure he is dear. Just a matter of time before his name is cleared I am sure of it.' Susie agreed.

Cecil finished off his cup of tea before declaring that he really must get going.

'Oh are you going somewhere?' Susie asked.

'Unfortunately yes, it's my mother!'

'Oh no what has happened?'

'She's not been well and has landed in hospital. So I have to head home to Salisbury for a few days.'

'Oh dear I hope she is alright?'

'She will be, but I really must get going!' he replied, 'lovely of you to visit though.'

With that he swept up the remaining cups and tea pot and placed them in the sink. Susie got the idea she had over stayed her welcome. She told Cecil she would show herself out and bid him farewell.

Back in her car she decided to linger for a moment. Sure enough a few minutes later Cecil jumped in his car, slammed the door shut, and then backed out of the driveway. She watched as he put the car in drive and then took off down the street.

Susie contemplated following him to see where he was really going but decided against it. He did seem rather agitated today, and she didn't want to give him any reason to be upset with her.

The thing was she had thought to herself, she really couldn't predict Cecil Miller. He was a hard character to read.

'And why was he in such a hurry?' she asked out loud to herself. 'Was it really his mother?'

42

Back in the High Street in Polmerton Susie had a few errands she had to run. Mostly though she wanted to just hang around for when Irvine's friend the Barrister would arrive. She wondered if she might follow along in the background and see what she could find out.

It seemed to her that the local police were unlikely to be any match for a high paid sophisticated London Barrister. He was probably going to run rings around them and get poor Irvine out on a technicality. The Inspector, despite the level of guilt he felt Irvine might have, would be forced to release him from the lock up pending further investigation. So she suspected Irvine would be free to go shortly after his friend's arrival.

Susie visited Hunter in the bakery and they made small talk for a while in between customers.

The whole time though she kept one eye and ear to the street in case the Barrister turned up. She was sure it wouldn't be hard to pick him out in Polmerton. No doubt he would have big city written all over him.

Susie was chatting with Aimee when the door opened and a customer walked in. It was Mrs Pettlebottom who greeted them all with delight.

'Hello again dear,' she said to Susie.

'Nice to see you Mrs Pettlebottom,' Susie returned the greeting.

Mrs Pettlebottom explained that she didn't often come into Polmerton to do her shopping but she just had to make the trip. Apparently word had gotten out about these new delicacies the Famous Polmerton Bakery were making. A sponge cake dipped in chocolate and coconut from Australia she informed Susie.

'You don't say?' Susie said acting like she hadn't yet sampled them.

'Oh yes, every one is raving about them!'

'I must give them a try,' Susie agreed.

'Bring some when you next come for tea with Mrs Brown then,' Mrs Pettlebottom suggested.

She paid Aimee the money owed for her two loathes of bread, and a tray of the lamingtons.

'Yes I must call again soon,' Susie said.

'Indeed she would welcome the company no doubt,' Mrs Pettlebottom said, 'She hasn't been the same since he left her at the…'

She didn't get to finish her sentence. She was interrupted by a shouting match out on the footpath directly outside the bakery. Two men were exchanging heated words, and it sounded like it was about to get physical.

'I'll go for the police then,' Hunter said and opened the door of the shop and stepped outside. The volume of the argument went up exponentially causing Susie, Aimee and Mrs Pettlebottom to all file out onto the street to witness the commotion.

'The barrister!' Aimee exclaimed.

He was an immaculately groomed gentleman in his early fifties. His tailored suit was made from a quality fabric and was a dark grey with navy blue pin stripe through it. His shirt tailored to fit his athletic physique and finished to perfection with gold cuff links. On top of his head his golden locks of hair combed to one side in the latest fashion from London. The barrister was clearly a man who was confident in how he presented himself and was not one to back down from an argument.

Susie wasn't surprised to see that the offending person he was deep in the argument with was none other than the Inspector.

As she had predicted the barrister had arrived and immediately demanded the release of his client Irvine Maxwell. He claimed that the missing rifle had been stolen from the home of Irvine Maxwell and Cecil Miller. The police themselves having a written record of the occasion from when Cecil Miller called them to report the theft himself three weeks ago.

The barrister claimed that there was no evidence to suggest the rifle was the one that was used to kill Mr Foley. Even if it had been, which it wasn't, there was still no evidence that would justify locking up his client.

Not too pleased at being made to look the fool the Inspector had stood up and imposed his bulk over the barrister. Susie surmised that the barrister must have taken a few backwards steps out the door of the police station to their current position.

'I demand you let my client go this instance!' the barrister cried for all the gathered crowd to hear.

'You can demand all you like but right now he is the number one suspect!'

'Well that is just ridiculous and you know it! There is no way that my client could have done it!'

The Inspector was becoming agitated by the situation. Susie noticed him cast his glance around the group that had gathered to see what on earth was going on? His face was bright red and perspiration ran down the side of his face.

'And why is that then?' the Inspector cried at the Londoner.

'Because he was sitting in the front row at the time, the shot was fired you fool!'

A hush came over the gathered folks.

'That's right he was I remember!' Mrs Pettlebottom said, 'he was sitting in front of me at the time!'

'There you go!' the barrister said turning and pointing to Mrs Pettlebottom, 'a witness who says it was impossible for him to have done it!'

'But Cecil Miller wasn't!' Mrs Pettlebottom added.

Another hush came over the crowd. They all started thinking the same thing and looking at one another. Susie heard someone ask if Cecil could have really done it. The reply came back in the affirmative.

'It was Cecil Miller!' a voice shouted out.

'Must have been Cecil,' another voice called from behind Susie.

'There you go,' the barrister said in a loud resonate voice for all to hear, 'sounds like you have the wrong man! Cecil Miller is the one you want!'

The Inspector folded his arms and let out a snort of disgust. The crowd, now numbering around twenty, hushed waiting for his response.

'Isn't Cecil Miller also your client?' the Inspector calmly asked.

Laughter erupted at the statement. The barrister for a brief moment had been caught off guard. He had briefly forgotten that both Irvine and Cecil were his clients and good friends. Susie noticed his brief moment of embarrassment before he regained his composure.

'That's not for us to determine. What we must sort out is you are detaining my client illegally without solid grounds to do so.'

The exchange was interrupted by the police door opening again. Out came Constable Daniels carrying a printed report. He was waving it trying to get the Inspectors attention.

'Yes well if I had my way, I would have them both locked up!' the Inspector said.

'You would what?' cried the barrister, 'is this some kind of homophobic law enforcement strategy down here in Cornwall?'

The crowd laughed again at the idea.

The inspector was furious at having his integrity questioned and started screaming back at the barrister before he was interrupted by Constable Daniels pushing past the crowd and in between the two warring parties.

Susie took a step back in case things got out of control.

'I don't think it was Irvine Maxwell!' the Constable shouted at the top of his voice.

'You what lad?' the Inspector asked glaring at the Constable.

'Here read this!' he handed the Inspector the report he had just printed off.

The report had just been filed by the forensics team. After conducting tests on both the rifle and the bullet they had come to the conclusion that there was no possibility that there was a match.

'What?' the Inspector said out loud.

'It says that the bullet isn't...'

'Yes I know full well what it says lad!' the Inspector said.

The Inspector turned and walked back to the police station. The barrister came after him demanding to know what was in the report. Once inside the Inspector took a seat as he shook his head in disbelief.

'Well?' the barrister said standing in the middle of the station with his hands on his hips.

The Inspector told Constable Daniels to release the prisoner, but to warn him that further questions would need to be asked so he was not to leave town.

Five minutes later Irvine Maxwell and the London barrister walked out of the police station into the salty fresh air. A small group of folks still in the street cheered them. Irvine gave them a brief wave and a few air kisses before being bundled into the waiting car of the barrister.

With the commotion now over and relative calm returned to the street Susie decided to head over to see Patty.

She found her at the end of the bar with a beer soaked rag over her shoulder. A handful of locals sat on their perch at the other end of the bar. They were busy gossiping about the street brawl the Inspector had just been involved in.

'Patty I wonder if I might have a word?' Susie said in a hurry.

'Of course, aye?'

'The police have just let their number one suspect go!' Susie stated feeling breathless.

'Yes I just saw the commotion!'

'Well the thing is, I don't think they have anything to go on right now.'

'That's a shame that is, and to think the killer is still on the loose!'

'Oh I know, that's why I wanted to enlist your help if I may?'

Patty agreed to help after Susie revealed her grand plan to her. She said that the only way they might get to the bottom of who killed Mr Foley was to re-enact the scene. To gather all the crew and cast together and place them in the same positions and live out the scene again. That way they might be able to think of an angle as to who did it and how. From there they might at least be able to find the murder weapon.

She asked Patty if it would be okay to organise it all for tomorrow night.

Patty of course readily agreed. She was as keen to get to the bottom of the matter as anyone. She told Susie it had been bad for business as no one wanted to go where people got murdered. So naturally she was keen to help.

'I'm not sure it will help much though, mind!' Patty said.

'Maybe it won't dear, but it's all we have to go on right now,' Susie said.

43

Susie & Meg had spent most of the next day on the phone. They had called everyone who was involved in the production of 'Castaways' to ask if they would join them at the Smugglers Inn tomorrow night at 6pm. Susie had instructed Meg not to let on the reason why.

She went over her plan again and again in her mind. She wanted to make sure she had every detail right, so she spent some time going through each detail of the case as she understood it. The success of her plan hinged on everyone being willing to join them. If key people did not attend, then the whole plan would not work.

Her biggest concern with her plan was how to deal with the Inspector. The last thing she wanted to do was to get offside with him.

She decided that she needed to involve him and make him feel like he played a pivotal role in catching the murderer.

'Right how did you go?' Susie asked Meg.

'Good, I've called everyone except for Cecil Miller. I can't get a hold of him.'

'Oh I think he has gone to see his sick mother,' Susie said.

Susie thought it best to call Irvine herself. A short while later she had him on the phone and explained the situation. Is there any way he could get Cecil to return for the night Susie had asked him?

Irvine agreed he would do his best. He wasn't sure how his mother was but to count on them both being there.

Later that day Susie nervously looked at her watch. It was 5:30pm and time to go. She wanted to be the first to arrive on the scene. With Meg by her side they jumped in the Land Rover and headed into town for their night at the Smugglers Inn.

Patty Malone greeted them and showed them out the back. She assured Susie that the theater room was unchanged from opening night.

Susie took a moment to walk up onto the stage and look out into the empty hall. The chairs had all been stacked away, so she asked Meg to put out two rows in the front. As Meg went about the unloading of chairs, Susie surveyed the stage area.

The props were all still on stage. The large pirate ship cutout as the backdrop. The treasure chest in the corner with the rusty anchor. The captains parrot in a bird cage hanging in the far corner.

To stage right was a table where props were placed. The gun used by Karl Lightfoot had been returned by the police at the time the rifle was found. She looked at it and a cold chill went down her spine.

Behind the table was the area Janet Brown used for costumes. A rack holding both the pirates and wenches costumes was still there. Surrounding that was Janet's work bench and sewing equipment. Behind the bench were large rolls of the most beautiful fabric. Lots of lovely colours and textures. Susie walked over and felt the texture of one fabric between her thumb and fingers. It was a delight to touch with a soft velvet texture that Susie loved.

Susie was interrupted by the arrival of Karl Lightfoot. He was looking better she thought and perhaps had gotten over the depressed state he was in. He greeted Susie and Meg and took a seat in the front row.

Mandy came in and said high. She was working the bar but said she would pop back in when Susie needed her. Patty also passed on the message she would join them. There was a new girl working behind the bar who could cover them both.

Janet Brown and Mrs Pettlebottom arrived together. Janet gave Susie a big hug. Her eyes were puffy and red and she looked like she had been crying. Mrs Pettlebottom kindly helped her find a seat.

There was small talk among those who had gathered. Several others arrived along with Hunter McGill who had brought supper for them all. Patty and Mandy had set up a table with a large urn and cups of tea for everyone.

'What's all this then?' the Inspectors voice boomed. It echoed around the hall which amplified the sound. Susie welcomed the Inspector and Constable Daniels. She took the Inspector to one side to explain the situation to him.

At first he had a look of great concern. He informed Susie that she really shouldn't be meddling in police business and he was going to have to put his foot down. When she told him that she was going to hand the murderer to him on a silver platter, and make him look like the one who solved the murder, well he was happy to let it happen. But only on this occasion.

Finally Irvine Maxwell arrived followed by a rather upset looking Cecil Miller. Irvine was his usual flamboyant self smiling and hugging everyone. He seemed as jolly as he ever was and happy to see everyone.

Cecil on the other hand was not happy. He scowled at everyone and went and sat in a corner. Susie sensed that he wasn't happy that Irvine had made him come back to Cornwall for the night. She wondered how Irvine had pulled it off but was glad he did.

When everyone had gathered with cups of tea and scones Susie walked up on to the stage.

'Could I have your attention please,' she asked. The chatter in the room was rather loud as everyone gossiped and speculated on what they were all doing here. No one heard her plea for attention.

'Quiet!' the Inspector bellowed.

A hush came over the crowd. No one wanted to be on the end of an argument with the Inspector. Not after yesterdays display in the street.

'Thank you Inspector,' Susie said from the stage looking down on them all. 'And thank you all for coming.'

'Are you going to do a song and dance routine for us?' Irvine asked jokingly. It broke the tension of the moment and everyone laughed.

'Not today Irvine, I think my acting days are behind me.' Susie responded. 'I suspect though you are all wondering why I have you all gathered here tonight?'

There was unanimous agreement amongst the gathered group.

'Are we going to revive Castaways and give it another run?' Patty asked from the back.

'In a sense yes,' Susie agreed.

Discussion broke out amongst them. There were arguments both for and against the idea but it seemed the consensus was that most were in favour. Susie struggled to regain control of the meeting.

'Quiet you lot' the Inspector said again, 'Hush now and let Lady Carter say what's on her mind now!'

'Thank you Inspector,' Susie said, 'While the idea of reviving Castaways is a good one, that is not what we are here for tonight!'

There was an exchange of looks amongst the group. They had no idea what was going on or what Susie had planned for them this evening. Karl suggested it might be some sort of wake for Mr Foley who has yet to be buried.

Susie informed them it was not a wake for Mr Foley although the time for that was coming soon.

'The reason we are all here is two fold,' Susie said, 'firstly to re-enact the scene of the murder!'

'Oh god!' Janet Brown let out a sorrowful cry. She sobbed and mopped up her tears with an already soggy handkerchief. Mrs Pettlebottom comforted her and encouraged Susie to continue.

'I would ask that you all join me in recreating the scene in a moment so the Inspector may examine the scene and see what clues can be identified.'

They all agreed that it made sense to do so. It would have been impossible on the night as there was so much commotion and panic amongst the crowd when it was obvious what had happened.

'The second reason we are here is I believe we can then reveal who the real murderer is!' Susie said.

A hush came over them as Susie looked them all in the eye one by one.

'You mean the murderer is in this room?' asked Karl.

'Yes I believe so!'

44

Susie explained to them all that she wanted them to take their places on the stage, or in the audience in the same spot they would have been. It took a few minutes for everyone to get organized.

On stage stood Susie and Patty the two wenches, off to one side. Karl Lightfoot stood on the other side of the stage with the prop gun in hand. Janet took her position to the side of the stage in the costumes area.

Seated in the audience were Meg and Constable Daniels. Next to them Irvine and Cecil. Immediately behind Irvine sat Mrs Pettlebottom.

'Right now I think we can begin,' Susie said. A rush of adrenaline surged through her veins.

'Wait a minute now,' Karl interjected, 'we need someone to be Mr Foley or it won't seem proper.'

'Yes you are right!' Susie said. Everyone agreed that for the re-enactment to feel right then they would need someone to play the part of Mr Foley. One by one the eyes of those gathered fell on the Inspector.

'Inspector,' Susie asked, 'would you do the honour?'

Reluctantly he agreed to do so. There was a halfhearted round of applause as he walked up the stairs and across the stage. Susie suggested he would be best down on his knees as Mr Foley was moments before the crime.

'Okay let us commence,' Susie said.

Susie started by saying that at the precise moment that Karl Lightfoot pointed the gun and pulled the trigger Mr Foley, true to character, dropped into a fetal position on the floor. Susie nodded to Karl who took his cue.

He raised the gun at the Inspector and pulled the trigger. The bolt in the gun made a dull thudding noise. The Inspector needed no encouragement. He grabbed at his abdomen with both hands, let out a whimper, and fell into a fetal position. For added effect he gasped and rocked back and forward in simulated agony.

'Now it was obvious to all in the crowd that it was Mr Lightfoot was the one who fired the fatal shot!' Susie stated.

She explained that it was well known that Mr Lightfoot and Mr Foley were never the best of friends. They had many disagreements over the years, and Mr Lightfoot had been drinking heavily of late. She cited the cast and crew party as an example.

It was easy to assume, which everyone did, that he was the guilty party. Everyone saw him do it, and he had a good enough reason. Being an actor and one for making a dramatic statement this was a wonderful way to get the attention he should have received.

'Well he did do it didn't he?' Mrs Pettlebottom asked confused. As she watched the re-enactment memories of the night came flooding back to her. She was convinced all over again that Mr Lightfoot was the one.

'Not according to forensics no' Susie stated.

She shared with them that when the forensics team examined the bullet extracted from the body of Mr Foley, it was found that it had not come from the gun used as the prop.

'So it wasn't Mr Lightfoot then?' Mrs Pettlebottom asked.

'Well he was released from custody on the basis of the bullet not matching the gun, that doesn't mean he didn't do it. It just means he didn't do it with that gun!' the Inspector added from his position on the floor.

'Quite right Inspector,' Susie agreed.

Susie went on to talk about the next possibility. She mentioned Mandy and asked where she had gone. She was in the audience a moment ago but now had disappeared.

'Mandy get in here now love!' Patty shouted out scaring the life out of Susie.

'I think she just ran to the loo,' Meg suggested.

Susie decided to carry on without her. She told the story of how
Mr Foley had accumulated large gambling debts while in Hollywood.
And how those holding the debts were desperate to get their money
back. She shared with everyone how they had been menacing Mandy
and posed a threat to her if she didn't repay the money.

'How much was it then?' Karl asked.

'Three hundred thousand dollars!' Susie added.

A gasp came over the group.

'So it was the Americans who killed Mr Foley after all then?' Meg
asked from the front row.

'I don't think so no, though Mandy did lead us to believe that
might be the case!' Susie said.

The Inspector added it couldn't have been them as they didn't
arrive in the country until the day after the murder had taken place.
Their passport stamps indicated the date and time of their arrival.

'Where is Mandy?' Patty asked feeling a little agitated. 'She really
should be here for this!'

'Oh come to think of it,' Mrs Pettlebottom spoke up, 'She wasn't
in the hall at the moment of the murder either!'

Another gasp came over the room.

'Well we will get back to Mandy in a moment,' Susie said.

She explained that after a tea party with the Aunties, who returned
to her several books, she had her interest sparked in all things
Smugglers in the area. She explained that she visited Acton Castle
and spoke with the owner there. He had told her about the Carter
brothers and how they had used a tunnel from the cove right into the
castle itself.

'You see, one thing that always bothered me about the case,' Susie
said, 'was that forensics were telling us the murder weapon was a
rifle! The shorter more compact type used for hunting.'

'You mean the kind that Irvine and Maxwell have a collection of?'
Mr Lightfoot asked.

'Precisely yes!' Susie agreed.

The thing that had bothered her she went on was that it would
have been incredibly difficult to get a rifle in and out of the venue
without being spotted by someone. Someone must have seen
something.

It was at that moment that she realised the murderer must have
used the rumoured smugglers tunnel. She explained that while Patty

was reluctant to let people know about the tunnel because she didn't want to attract treasure hunters.

'And it was a risk to peoples safety!' Patty added. She nodded towards Susie who automatically reached up to feel the lump on her forehead. It had turned a nasty shade of purple and yellow. She had been explaining it away as having walked into a door.

'Yes it is!' Susie agreed.

She explained how she did some research and thanked both Patty and Janet Brown for their assistance. Convinced that the murderer had escaped out through the tunnel during the commotion at the end of the play, she had Constable Daniels explore the cellar below the stage area they were now standing on. He searched for both signs of a murder weapon, and the entrance to the tunnel, but found neither.

'Because that is not where the tunnel is!' Patty exclaimed.

'Yes and to get to the tunnel entrance with the rifle would have meant walking past a hundred or so people!' the Inspector said from his fetal position.

'So what happened?' asked Mrs Pettlebottom.

'Well after exploring the tunnel from the other side at the harbour,' Susie said.

'And getting trapped for an age!' added Meg. Susie smiled when she saw Constable Daniels squeeze her hand.

'Yes you are right,' Susie agreed, 'my foolishness meant we were trapped in the tunnel until the brave Constable came along.'

She told the story of how on the way out it was touch and go with the tide rushing in, but they eventually escaped. Only Max had found something hidden wrapped up in an old rag. On pulling it out we found a hunting rifle which belonged to Irvine Maxwell.

'How do you know it was his then?' Karl asked.

'Because it had a badge on it with the initials IM!' replied Constable Daniels.

All eyes fell on Irvine Maxwell. He nodded and agreed it was his rifle.

'But Mr Maxwell sat right in front of me. He was right there when it happened!' Mrs Pettlebottom objected. She sounded annoyed that Mr Maxwell, whom she admired greatly, might be accused of such a horrendous act.

'Yes you are right dear!' Susie said from stage.

'Yes but Cecil Miller had left a few minutes before the shooting took place,' Mrs Pettlebottom added.

Another gasp from everyone as this new information came to light.

'Indeed he had,' Susie agreed, 'he left with just enough time before the final scene to come back stage, get in position, and fire the fatal shot. And no doubt he had the motive to do it having informed me several times that he would have killed Foley himself given half a chance!'

'So it was you then,' Mrs Pettlebottom said jabbing a bony finger into the back of his shoulder. 'You shot him and then hid the rifle in the tunnel hoping it would never be found!'

The Inspector got to his feet. Excitement and pleasure was written all over his face. Finally they had their man. 'Constable, arrest Mr Cecil Miller immediately!'

'Not so fast Inspector. You are forgetting something,' Susie said.

'Oh aye, what's that then?'

Susie asked Cecil to explain where he went moments before the fatal shooting. Cecil said he was the acting stage hand, so he went backstage to draw the curtain closed the moment the gun shot happened. And then to draw it back open when all the cast were lined up on stage to take a bow.

'Besides which, forensics report showed the bullet did not come from Irvine Maxwells rifle after all!'

Everyone sighed with confusion. They had arrived at a point where they had no real idea who it might have been who killed Mr Foley.

'So who was it then?' Karl asked getting frustrated.

'Well this is when I got the big break through in the case. It seemed very odd to me that the rifle which had previously been reported stolen by Cecil, would turn up in the smugglers tunnel right after I had been making enquiries about the existence of such a tunnel.'

'And it was placed where it would be found too!' Meg added.

'Oh yes that does seem odd!' Mrs Pettlebottom agreed.

'Yes, it almost seemed like someone had planted the rifle there in order to have the evidence point to Irvine Maxwell. It was almost like whoever put it there was trying to point the finger of blame at Mr Maxwell which almost worked.'

'You don't say!' the Inspector said trying to put all the pieces together in his mind.

Susie explained that from the moment she realised this the question changed. She went from asking who murdered Mr Foley and how, to who might want to set up Mr Irvine Maxwell and make him look like a murderer.

'And who was it then?' Karl asked.

'Well the most obvious person was you Mr Lightfoot!' Susie said. She explained that he had been overheard on several occasions fighting with Mr Maxwell about never getting the lead role. What better way to show your disappointment than to kill the Hollywood star, who was the apple of Mr Maxwell's eye, and then make it look like Mr Maxwell himself did it.

Karl Lightfoot laughed like a crazy man at the idea.

'Go on then,' he encouraged her to continue.

Everyone went silent as she explained of course it wasn't Mr Lightfoot, and that there was only possible person who it could have been when you consider all the evidence.

'So it's obvious then who the real killer is,' Susie said, 'Inspector would you now reveal who murdered Mr Foley!'

45

The Inspector stood and brushed his coat from the dust. Everything slowed down in his mind and he felt the weight of all the eyes in the room upon him. He was trying to piece together everything Susie had just said and work out her train of thought, but he was coming up blank.

'Yes, right well I shall do that!' he said and turned slowly to face Susie.

Susie recognised immediately that he had no real idea of what she had been talking about. His face was a blank, and he risked making a fool of himself. She sighed. She had tried to get him involved and make it look like his brilliant police work, but it was too no avail.

'The murderer is…' he paused hoping inspiration would strike him. It didn't and his face shifted from blank to distressed.

'Before you reveal the murderer Inspector,' Susie interjected, 'I think I should sum up the facts as we know them!'

Everyone agreed a good summary would help at this point.

Susie explained that the murderer had to have been someone with a strong motive to do so, but they also would have had to have had access to the side of the stage at the right moment. In addition, they would need a way to get the rifle in and out of the theater that's if the rifle ever actually left the theater itself.

At that moment the door to the hall swung open and Mandy came rushing in.

'Sorry everyone,' Mandy said and took her seat next to Meg.

All eyes immediately shifted to Mandy, and then back to Susie, then back to Mandy.

Further to this Susie explained that the person responsible not only wanted to kill Mr Foley, but they also wanted to try to frame Irvine Maxwell.

'So that can only leave one person who fits the bill!' Susie declared.

Again all the eyes fell on Mandy. She shifted uncomfortably in her seat.

'Inspector?' Susie asked, hoping that the sum up would lead him to the killer.

Again his face was blank.

She frantically nodded her head to the left of stage. He looked, and he still didn't get it. He turned to her and shrugged his shoulders.

Susie stepped forward.

'It seems the cat has the Inspectors tongue,' Susie said.

'Wait just a minute,' the Inspector declared, 'I believe I know who the murderer is now!'

He beamed a wide smile at Susie. Everyone was on the edge of their seats.

'The murderer was…'

'Yes exactly, it was you Janet Brown!' Susie said finishing off the sentence. Susie was sure he was about to say Mandy and she couldn't let that happen.

A hush came over the crowd. It was the last person they all suspected.

She let out a wale of sadness and threw herself to her knees.

'And I believe Mrs Brown, the rifle is right there in your sewing area is it not?'

Janet was on her knees weeping.

Constable Daniels and the Inspector headed to the sewing area and begun searching frantically but no rifle was to be found.

'Check inside the rolls of material!' Susie said.

She explained to everyone that she believed Mrs Brown had brought the rifle in to the theater in a roll of material. She fired the rifle over Mr Lightfoot's shoulder at the precise moment. In the commotion she hid the rifle back into the roll of material and left it there knowing that it would be the last place anyone would search.

'But why?' Karl asked in disbelief.

'I loved him!' she cried out, 'but he left me at the altar because of his sordid affair with Irvine Maxwell!'

Everyone in the room gasped and held their breath.

'I couldn't let Irvine take him away from me so I did what any woman would do in my position. For years he promised to marry me and the very day it was finally to happen he didn't turn up at the church. No, I found him drunk in bed with Irvine Maxwell!'

The Inspector found the roll of material that contained the rifle and slid it out into the open stage area.

Constable Daniels found his handcuffs and cuffed her hands behind her back. Tears ran down her face in a sad reflection of what her life had become.

Susie felt terrible. She really didn't feel that Janet was a bad person in her heart, but there is no telling how far someone will go when you keep pushing them to the edge and leaving them there.

'Right oh then, as I suspected,' the Inspector said, 'best take you in for a few questions.'

Everyone watched as Inspector Reynolds and Constable Daniels led Janet out of the hall.

46

The next morning Hunter dropped by the castle and delivered a lovely batch of fresh Cornish delights. Susie was in the garden so he gave her a wave as he carried in the tray. He found Woolsworth who took possession of the tray and carried it to the kitchen.

'Oh the garden is looking lovely!' Hunter declared walking over to Susie. Max got up from his position in the shade under the old oak tree. He wondered over to Hunter hoping for a treat but happy to settle for a pat.

'Thank you dear,' Susie said from her position on the ground. She had on gardening gloves and her old clothes. She was covered from head to toe in the garden and had a smear of mud across her forehead where she had tried to wipe away the sweat from her brow.

'Oh I must look a mess!' she apologised.

'Not at all Susie,' Hunter beamed his usual jolly smile at her, 'you look as lovely as ever.'

Susie blushed. She was not used to being on the receiving end of such generous compliments.

'Thank you kind sir,' she smiled back at him.

He told her he had dropped off a tray of delights for the morning tea party with the Aunties. Susie asked him if he would stay for it but he had a few things to do first thing. He suggested he might come back though around midday as they needed to discuss their plans for the words largest tea party.

'And how did you sleep after the events last night?' he asked her.

She told him that her, Meg and Mandy had stayed up until late watching the latest romantic comedies on TV. There was lots of wine drunk and chocolate consumed. It was a strange kind of night as on the one hand she was glad to close the lid on the whole murder business. For Mandy's sack if for no other reason. On the other hand she had grown rather fond of Janet Brown. She really didn't believe her to be a murderer as such. It was more of a case of acting out of grief she felt.

'Well I best be off, things to do,' he said and gave her a wink.

Susie got up and walked him to his car. She waved as he drove down the driveway and into the distance.

Half an hour later she was showered and changed. She could hear the Aunties in the entrance hall as she came down the stairs.

They were delighted as ever to see her. Greetings were exchanged all around. Max was excitedly wagging his tail and getting pat's where ever he could. They asked after the whereabouts of Meg. Susie told them that Meg and Mandy had gone into town to organise the funeral. They would be back shortly to join them for morning tea.

'Why don't we take tea out in the rotunda this morning?' Susie suggested and led the way. It was a beautiful sunny day, with a soft gentle breeze making its way up from the ocean below them. The rotunda was Susie's favourite place to sit and relax.

Woolsworth brought them a large tray of tea pots, cups and saucers, along with milk jugs and sugar. After a brief exchange of pleasantries he returned inside to fetch the tray of delights that Hunter had brought.

The tray left a trail of exotic smelling goodness wafting behind it. Max followed along behind sniffing the air. They all laughed, except for Woolsworth, at the sight.

'Now you must tell us all about last night?' Mable said sitting up to pay attention.

'Yes indeed, we hear you got your man at last,' Mildred said.

'In a manner of speaking dear,' Mable clarified.

'Yes do tell us everything!' Mildred said.

Susie proceeded to tell them all in great detail how the night at the Smugglers Inn had unfolded. She started with her giving instructions to Meg to call everyone and make sure they could attend. To her surprise they managed to get all the key people there.

'Even Inspector Reynolds was keen as he was clearly lost with this case,' Susie told them.

'He does need a little encouragement now and then,' Mabel said. It caused laughter all around.

Susie went on and explained how through a process of elimination she was able to narrow down the field of suspects to just a couple of people who could have done it and had the motive to do it.

She told the Aunties that what had puzzled her was when they discovered it was a rifle that was the murder weapon. It was almost impossible to bring it into the theater and leave with it, without being seen. The Aunties both agreed that did pose a sticking point.

'Then when you returned the book 'Smugglers Guide to Cornwall' to me it got me thinking,' Susie said. The Aunties where on the edge of their seats as she told them she investigated the idea of the murderer using a smugglers tunnel to escape after the shooting, or at least to hide the rifle.

'But didn't you find the rifle in the tunnel?' Mable asked confused.

'Yes, that is what we heard!' Mildred agreed.

'Yes it was Mr Maxwell's, was it not?' Mable asked.

Susie confirmed that they did indeed find the rifle in the cave entrance. That was when she started to look at the case differently. She said it was obvious to her that the rifle had been planted there. After Patty showed her the real entrance to the tunnel from the Smugglers Inn, she had realised there was no way the murderer had used it. So for the gun to turn up at the harbour side of the tunnel made it very suspicious.

'So I was convinced that the rifle was planted there for us to find,' Susie explained.

'You don't say?' Mable gasped.

'Who would do that though?' Mildred asked.

'Good question,' Susie said, 'that is the question I started asking myself. Why would someone plant Irvine Maxwell's rifle in the cave for us to find it?'

'Obviously to frame Mr Maxwell!' Mable stated boldly.

'Precisely!' Susie agreed, 'That is when I stopped looking for who killed Mr Foley, and started looking for who wanted to frame Mr Maxwell for the murder.'

'Which led you to Janet Brown then?'

'Yes well it was something the two of you said when last you were here,'

'Oh really. Do tell?' Mabel said with delight. Mabel and Mildred exchanged a look of satisfaction between them.

'Yes, when you told me that Janet and Mr Foley were an item it all just made sense. She couldn't stand the thought of losing him to Irvine Maxwell. So she tried to kill two birds with one stone so to speak!'

'Oh that all makes sense now!' Mable said.

Mildred nodded in agreement.

'Poor dear!' Susie sighed.

47

The Aunties had to head home earlier than expected. They told Susie all about the renovations they had planned for their new kitchen. They wanted a more modern look with a larger stove and more expansive basins.

They had both recently taken a Thai cooking course online and suggested to Susie that she must come over one night for dinner. Susie agreed it was a terrific idea, and a date was set for the following week.

She bid them farewell and watched them drive away down the winding drive. They passed Hunter on the way up to see Susie. She saw him approach, so she went inside to her office and found the folder Meg had put together for her. The folder had all the information and plans for the 'Worlds Largest Tea Party' that she was planning with Hunter. Inside were costings, and quotes from suppliers, along with a detailed plan of where to place tables and marques in the lawns of the castle.

Now that the messy business of the killing of Mr Foley was behind them she was glad to have something positive and fun to look forward to.

Hunter and Susie took a seat in the rotunda as Woolsworth cleared the table from the visit with the Aunties.

'Goodness you are just going from one morning tea to another,' Hunter laughed.

'Yes and with all the treats I am eating in between I will need a proper diet plan soon!' Susie said.

They spent the next ten minutes going over the map that Meg had prepared. Hunter informed Susie that in order to beat the record for the 'Worlds Largest Tea Party' they would need to accommodate about 350 people. The problem was with the map that Meg had drawn out they could only realistically fit in about 200 people.

'Oh dear!' Susie said not having realised how many people exactly they would need.

They talked about opening up the lower paddocks which would easily hold five hundred people on its own. Susie said that she had leased the lower paddocks of about twenty acres to Mr Charleston, a farmer from over near St Ives. He was running a small herd of sheep in the paddocks, but she didn't think he would mind.

'Perhaps we could have the dignitaries and local folks from the business community in the upper section around the castle and open the lower paddocks up to the public?' suggested Hunter.

Susie thought it was a workable idea. She did have one criteria though. She wanted to make sure the event would cover its own costs, and both raise money for repairs to the castle and also raise money for a charity.

'Sounds grand, did you have a charity in mind?' Hunter asked knowing she most likely did.

'Yes as a matter of fact I do,' Susie smiled.

Meg and her had been discussing the idea of supporting Pink Ribbon, a charity that was focused on raising awareness of breast cancer prevention, and finding a cure. They were both passionate about the idea as both Meg and Susie had known friends in the past to suffer with breast cancer.

'Oh a great idea,' Hunter said as his mind started to move into overdrive. 'Perhaps we could have everyone wear pink on the day?'

'Wonderful! I would love to see the castle decked out in pink!'

Woolsworth delivered them a fresh tray of tea and some ham and cheese sandwiches. Susie asked him his opinion of the idea of the tea party and having the castle a wash of pink in support of the Pink Ribbon Foundation.

He simply smiled and raised his trouser legs to reveal pink socks.

'Many people are not aware Ma'am, but men can also get breast cancer!' he informed them.

'Is that right? I had no idea!' replied Susie.

'Yes Ma'am! Your uncle Charles first got ill with breast cancer. That developed into more insidious forms of cancer later on which led to him departing us.'

'That's decided then!' Hunter said, 'It will be a day for both men and women!'

Susie and Woolsworth agreed it was a fine idea.

Woolsworth went to dust and left them to the planning of the day. Susie and Hunter chatted for the next hour making plans. They made up lists of who was to do what and by when. They both agreed that their first port of call was to get the Pink Ribbon Foundation on board.

Susie could imagine the main tower of the castle wrapped in a gigantic pink ribbon, and a large pink ribbon wrapping around the outer walls of the castle. She laughed and told Hunter she had no idea how such things might happen, but she was sure Meg could handle it without a problem.

They talked about getting the media involved along with a range of sponsors.

'Of course the Cornwall Cooking School will be an automatic sponsor!' Hunter stated.

'Yes and I think with all the work you are putting into it, that the Famous Polmerton Bakery should also be a sponsor.' Susie suggested.

They decided they would be Silver Sponsors of the event and open it up to local business to become additional Silver Sponsors. For larger corporate they could be Gold Sponsors for a healthy sum. It was agreed there would be just three Gold Sponsors for the event.

'Well it sounds like we have a workable plan now then!' Hunter said.

They were so engrossed in their planning that they hadn't heard Meg arrive home. She had been inside and changed and now wandered down to the rotunda to say hello to them both.

Meg was over joyed with excitement. She told them she was going on a proper date with Constable Daniels. They had planned a picnic on the foreshore, then a movie later at the Newlyn Filmhouse, followed by a dinner at the Boathouse Restaurant in Penzance.

'A proper date at last!' squealed Meg with delight.

'Oh that's wonderful news,' Susie said, her face smiling with joy for her. 'When is he picking you up then?'

'In half an hour!' Meg said. Realising she didn't have long to get ready she bid them farewell and rushed off to shower and change.

'Young love,' Susie sighed watching her run off, 'isn't it grand!'

'Love at any age is grand Susie!' Hunter smiled at her.

48

Susie had a light tea of pumpkin soup and toast. The soup was spiced with a little curry powder and chilli. It was the perfect light meal for a cold night. Thankfully Woolsworth had lit the fire, and she had curled up on the sofa with Max by her side.

She was excited about the coming Worlds Largest Tea Party and loved working in partnership with Hunter. For a while she thought about what a good man Hunter was and how she enjoyed his company. Then she snapped herself out of it.

'Think it's time I called Margery!' she declared to Max. He gave a bark at the sound of her name. She was always good to him bringing him treats whenever she would visit.

She went into the office and found the phone. Meg had changed the batteries on it yesterday so she could wander around the castle and still be able to make calls. Returning to the sofa she had to nudge Max to make room. He had taken advantage of her absence and spread out.

For the next hour she chatted with Margery. They talked mostly about the murder of Mr Foley and how poor Janet Brown found no other option but to kill him and try to frame Mr Maxwell. Margery listened with fascination as Susie recalled every detail.

Margery marvelled at how Susie was able to solve the murder when the police were stuck without a clue. She always thought Susie had missed her calling in life and perhaps might have been better suited to a life solving crime.

Susie joked that she didn't really like spending time with criminals to which they both roared with laughter. Margery thought that at the very least she should be on the payroll and she had a good mind to tell the Inspector so.

After chatting about the murder talk soon got to the Worlds Largest Tea Party.

Margery loved the idea and especially using it as a way to support the Pink Ribbon Foundation. She asked Susie how she could get involved.

Plans were soon made for Margery to come and stay with them a week before the grand event.

'And stay as long as you like dear,' Susie said, 'it will be so great to have your company for a while!'

'Oh I might just move in then!'

There was more laughter and catching up on all the latest gossip.

They bid each other farewell just as car lights were seen coming up the driveway.

Susie told Max that it was most likely to be Constable Daniels dropping Meg off.

Sure enough ten minutes later after a number of good bye kisses in the car, Meg emerged and came inside. She found Susie and Max curled up on the sofa.

'You two sure look cosy!' Meg said. She had a smile that lit up the room though she tried to hide it.

Max tried to wag his tail with happiness at seeing Meg, but he was sitting on it. The result was he just wiggled his backside a little.

'Well?' Susie asked, 'How was it?'

Meg smiled some more looking rather coy.

Then she thrust her hand forward to reveal a sparkling bright diamond ring.

'We're getting married!' she squealed with excitement.

Susie leapt to her feet, tears of happiness streaming down her face.

They hugged each other tight and Susie kissed her on the cheek. Both of them wiping tears from their eyes.

'Show me now?' Susie said.

Meg held out her hand and Susie took in the beauty of the engagement ring.

'How wonderful!' Susie said overcome with joy.

'Isn't it just,' Meg agreed, 'and there is something I want to ask you?'

'Go on then?'

'Will you give me away?' Meg asked with hope.

'Oh, of course dear!'

They chatted about the future and what plans they had made.

Susie suggested that they have the wedding here at Ash Castle. Meg clapped her hands in delight. She said that they had talked about asking her if they could get married at the castle.

They both went to bed that night dreaming of a fairy tale wedding.

—— The End ——

ABOUT THE AUTHOR

Jessica Moore is the pen name of an Australian Mystery & Thriller author. After visiting Cornwall in 2010 she fell in love with the charms of the quaint seaside villages and gorgeous countryside. Growing up as a child she was fascinated with castles and pirates. Today Jessica is busy writing more books in the Susie Carter Mystery series.

SUSIE CARTER MYSTERY SERIES

Murder At Ash Castle
Pirates, Wenches & Murder
Tea Party Murder

Join the newsletter & get notified as each book
is released ahead of release date:

www.JessicaMoore.me

Printed in Poland
by Amazon Fulfillment
Poland Sp. z o.o., Wrocław

90506001R00127